P9-DGP-852

IRVING ROBBINS MIDDLE SCHOOL
LIBRARY MEDIA CENTER
WOLF PIT ROAD
FARMINGTON, CT 06034-1127

Norby and the Terrified Taxi

Other titles in the Norby Series
by Janet and Isaac Asimov

Norby and the Mixed-up Robot
Norby's Other Secret
Norby and the Lost Princess
Norby and the Invaders
Norby and the Queen's Necklace
Norby Finds a Villain
Norby Down to Earth
Norby and Yobo's Great Adventure
Norby and the Oldest Dragon
Norby and the Court Jester

Books on Robots

How Did We Find Out About Robots? (Isaac Asimov)
Mind Transfer (Janet Asimov)
The Package in Hyperspace (Janet Asimov)

NORBY AND THE TERRIFIED TAXI

Janet Asimov

Walker and Company
New York

Copyright © 1997 by Janet Jeppson Asimov

All rights reserved. No part of this book may be reproduced or transmitted in any form or by any means, electronic or mechanical, including photocopying, recording, or by any information storage and retrieval system, without permission in writing from the Publisher.

All the characters and events portrayed in this work are fictitious.

First published in the United States of America in 1997 by Walker Publishing Company, Inc.

Published simultaneously in Canada by Thomas Allen & Son Canada, Limited, Markham, Ontario

Library of Congress Cataloging-in-Publication Data
Asimov, Janet.
Norby and the terrified taxi/Janet Asimov.
p. cm.
Summary: Jeff and Norby travel to Earth where a Manhattan taxi with a robot brain helps them investigate Garc the Great's connection with Computer Prime.
ISBN 0-8027-8642-1
[1. Robots—Fiction. 2. Taxicabs—Fiction. 3. Science fiction.]
I. Title
PZ7.A836Nnae 1997
[Fic]—DC21 97-3583
CIP AC

Printed in the United States of America

2 4 6 8 10 9 7 5 3 1

For Beth Walker.
And in memory of Sam.

Contents

Norby and the
Terrified Taxi

1

Time Travel Trouble

"Now hear this, Cadet Jefferson Wells. That mixed-up robot of yours has bungled again!" The deep bass voice boomed out of the ship's intercom.

Jeff had been trying to comb back his curly, dark brown hair, to hide the fact that he'd forgotton to get a haircut, but at the sound of Admiral Yobo's voice he ran to the guest cabin to find the majestic chief of Space Command wearing a ferocious scowl, regulation pants, and nothing from the waist up.

The Wells brothers' ship, optimistically named *The Hopeful*, shook as Boris Yobo stamped his foot and pointed to a thoroughly shredded article of clothing. "That's the tunic of my best dress uniform, Jeff!"

"I'm sorry, sir. Norby meant well. He knew you were in a hurry so he beefed up the laundry computer a little. Perhaps you could just wear your second-best . . ."

Yobo growled. "My second-best tunic has unaccountably become somewhat—ah—snug. I will have to go out of uniform."

As Jeff wondered whether that meant going half naked, Yobo pulled an exotically gold-patterned tunic over his well-muscled black torso.

"That looks fine, Admiral. It will be perfect for late spring in Manhattan."

"Humph!" Yobo stalked out of the cabin with Jeff in pursuit. "I hope you Wells brothers realize that the Solar Federation calls upon my Space Command to solve even the smallest of its problems and that I'm making a large sacrifice by visiting Earth now."

When they entered the control room, no one else was there.

1

"Well, where are that little monster of a robot and your rascal of a brother, who's responsible for taking me from my duties just when I'm needed? What's taking them so long to finish a simple task of finding a prankster?"

"A what?"

"Someone who perpetrates pranks, Cadet. These have been mainly minor annoyances, like graffiti on government structures or cartoon faces appearing at the bottom of official documents." Yobo tapped his broad chin. "But it wasn't so minor when Luna City's computer went momentarily haywire and dumped garbage into the excavation site of the new opera house."

"Sort of funny . . ."

"Cadet!"

"Sorry, sir. Here they come, Admiral." In the viewscreen, Jeff could see two figures enter the transparent enclosed walkway that connected *The Hopeful*'s dock to the huge rotating wheel of Space Command's headquarters, in permanent orbit around Mars.

The tall, black-haired human was Yobo's secret agent and Jeff's older brother, Farley Gordon Wells. Fargo's usually cheerful face was glum, his blue eyes solemn.

The other figure was a small, rotund robot keeping up with Fargo's long strides only by elevating on his personal miniantigrav instead of walking with his short legs. Norby had obviously polished his silvery barrel of a body to a fine glow in honor of the trip they were about to make.

"No luck?" asked Yobo when they came through the airlock.

Fargo shrugged. "All I know is that the culprit had to be outside to do the job. . . ."

"That means the culprit's a robot!" Yobo glared at Norby.

"Not me, sir!" Norby made a noise like the grinding of metal teeth, except that he didn't have any teeth. In his half a head, under the brim of his domed metal hat, both his front and back sets of eyes blinked rapidly, which meant that his emotive circuits were agitated.

Fargo sat down at the control panel. "You're right, Admiral. The culprit was indeed a robot. We traced it through the paint, a common type that can be bought anywhere, but a little different from the regulation stuff used by Space Command."

"Well, what robot defaced the space side of my headquarters with red paint?"

"We found the paint container still hooked on to one of the small magnetic robots that cleans the outer hull."

"Impossible. The very small brains of cleaning robots cannot be programmed to commit vandalism—there are too many built-in prohibitions. An additional brain component must have been added to the cleaning robot."

Norby jiggled on his two-way feet. "No, sir, I checked. It was an ordinary cleaning robot, with no memory of doing the vandalism. And since it could not have been programmed to do the job, someone must have been controlling it at the time, but I don't know how they made it do what it did. Nobody can control me that way."

"Unfortunately," said Yobo.

Jeff saw that Norby was beginning to jiggle faster, so he quickly asked, "Did you investigate any unregistered people here in Space Command or in passing ships?"

Fargo answered. "Sure. There's no evidence of anyone in a space suit being outside with the robot. The control had to come from within Space Command or from a ship, but everyone working in or stopping at Space Command seems to have had a legitimate reason for being here."

"Anyway," Norby continued stubbornly, "the control would have had to be highly unusual."

"That's worrisome," Yobo said. "I should stay and investigate this matter."

Fargo turned on *The Hopeful*'s minifusion motors. "Admiral, you promised you'd go with me on this trip."

"Yet it's possible that these pranks are connected with the problem that Computer Prime picked up."

"Even that can wait a day, Admiral," said Fargo.

"What about Computer Prime?" asked Jeff, feeling a twinge of anxiety. Any computer could tap into Computer Prime, the Federation's main storage library, also used for correlating the knowledge in the millions of electronic libraries and in the cyberspace of the Solarweb. The Federation could do without Computer Prime, but only at great inconvenience.

"Considering the unrecorded adventures you and Norby have had, I suppose you can keep a secret, Cadet. Computer Prime itself has not been affected as far as we know, but there's something odd going on in the Solarweb—mostly silly messages cropping up where they shouldn't."

"Silly messages?"

"Like 'Take me to my leader.' "

"*My* leader?" Jeff asked. "Didn't old cartoons show aliens landing on Earth and saying, 'Take me to *your* leader'?"

"Indeed. The prankster is either an ignoramus or crazy. Or both. Whatever, I don't like it." Yobo cleared his throat. It sounded like a thunderstorm brewing. "I'll have to get back here as soon as possible. Let's get on with Fargo's blasted trip."

Fargo blinked. "I admit I'm the cause of this trip, Admiral, but there's no need to insult me."

"Sorry. I'm feeling harassed."

"Admiral, there's something else, which won't make you feel any better," Fargo said, eyeing Norby. "I had a difference of opinion with Norby about it."

The little robot's half a head sank into his barrel body so that only the tops of his eyes peeked out over the edge. He was in back of Jeff, who felt Norby's hand suddenly grab his, establishing a telepathic link.

—Jeff, it's only my opinion, and the Admiral won't . . .

—Norby, whatever it is, you'd better say it. This is the first time the Admiral gave you a specific job to do with Fargo.

4

Norby's head shot up to its full extent. "Admiral, I think these pranks could be linked to the thefts of microbubble brain components from robot factories all over the Solar Federation."

Yobo's dark face got darker. "No wonder Fargo argued with you! That's classified information, Cadet Robot!"

"To correlate information I merely tapped into—"

"Secret files!" Yobo seemed to swell with outrage. "Norby, you bypassed the security codes that protect Space Command's information and if you ever do it again, I'll remove your insides and use you as a garbage disposal unit."

"Relax, sir. I'm the only one who could do it. After all, I'm unique."

"And the most modest robot in the galaxy," said Fargo, backing *The Hopeful* out of the dock.

"Great galaxy," Yobo yelled. "More red paint!"

Jeff saw that on both sides of the empty dock, someone had painted the words "Connection *Now!*"

"Connection?" Yobo asked. "What connection? And what's that written at the bottom in small letters?"

"According to my superior robot vision," Norby said, "these graffiti are signed. Who is Garc the Great?"

"Never heard of him," Yobo said, "but now I feel assured that this prankster is only a stupid person exercising a large ego in doing ridiculous things. I can't believe he's the same one who managed to steal microbubble components."

"Computer," Fargo said to the one in the ship, "tie in with Computer Prime. Find references to Garc the Great."

"No references."

"Then let's go home to my beloved."

As the ship moved farther away from the giant wheel shape of Space Command, Jeff said, "If Garc the Great *is* the one who stole the robot brain parts, then he could be dangerous."

Yobo stroked his big chin thoughtfully. "Correct, Cadet. I don't like this Garc the Great. Childishly egotistical villains can be the worst—like certain villains we've known in the past, who tried to take over the Federation and almost succeeded."

"Garc is new," Fargo said.

"Then I'll keep hunting for him, in case he does turn power mad," said Yobo, pulling down his tunic.

Fargo had evidently heard from Norby about Yobo's best dress uniform, because he winked at Jeff and said, "By the way, Admiral, my beloved will be smitten by the sight of you in that splendid Afro-Martian tunic."

"Your Albany Jones does have good taste," Yobo said with a pleased smile.

Fargo seemed to be scrutinizing Jeff. "The holov reporters will undoubtedly notice that the sleeves of Jeff's dress uniform are too short."

"I can't help being nearly sixteen and still growing."

Jeff thought it was fine that his handsome brother was in love with a beautiful cop. Unfortunately, the beautiful cop was also the daughter of Manhattan's mayor, who—like most politicians—was prone to turn every occasion into a Public Event, complete with media coverage. The lack of privacy meant that Jeff couldn't invite to the occasion his friends who lived on other worlds he'd visited with Norby.

Although a few people knew about Norby's talents, fewer knew about those other worlds. For this particular Public Event, Fargo and Albany had reluctantly decided to invite only inhabitants of the Terran solar system.

As *The Hopeful* shot off into space, away from Mars and toward Earth, Fargo said, "Plug in, Norby. We'll soon be far enough away from Space Command for you to use your hyperdrive without anyone seeing us."

"I can't. Leo Jones is calling on hycom."

The viewscreen filled with the bushy-haired head of the mayor of Manhattan. "Hello, my friends. I've ordered Lizzie to wait on your Fifth Avenue roof to take you to Gracie Mansion. Don't let your ship squash her when you land."

6

"No, sir," Jeff said.

Yobo looked puzzled. "Lizzie? Oh—the taxi."

"She's smarter than most taxis and she's a person—like me," Norby said.

"I hope not," Yobo muttered, "or we may have trouble getting to the ceremony."

Leo Jones pursed his lips. "Don't even think of such a thing. My daughter is already upset because Fargo had to do a last-minute job for you, Admiral. I hope you'll hurry." The mayor's ruddy face disappeared.

Fargo grinned. "On to Earth. My beloved awaits."

Jeff liked Lizzie. Long ago the old spacer MacGillicuddy found alien robot parts on an asteroid and used them when he made Norby, bought much later by Jeff to be his teaching robot. Norby was equipped with great intelligence and alien talents, but Lizzie was only an old taxi who had been given an improved robot brain by MacGillicuddy.

"I'll be glad to see Lizzie," Fargo said, with a mischievous glance at Jeff. "Unlike *some* robots, Lizzie is always reliable."

"Well, I am too!" Norby yelled predictably.

"Plug in, Norby," Jeff ordered.

As his antenna inserted into the control board, Norby added, also predictably, "And I'm saving you all money because those land-based matter transporters are expensive and the Feds are rethinking their faulty hyperdrive invention. I contain alien metal so I alone can bypass the speed-of-light limit of normal space by taking your ship through hyperspace."

"Yes," said Fargo, "and you also don't know how you do it."

"That's just as well, because otherwise you'd probably tell the Fed scientists about me and they'd take me apart to find out how I conquer the dimensionless dimension of hyperspace. . . ."

"That will do, Norby," Yobo said. "Take us to Earth."

7

Norby's eyes were shut and the antenna from his hat, one end of it plugged into the control board, was vibrating like the plucked string of a harp.

Jeff said, "What's the matter, Norby?"

Norby's left hand reached back to touch Jeff.

—It feels as if someone's hunting . . . maybe me!

—What? Who? Why?

—Don't know, Jeff. Someone with strange power, trying to make me part of something . . . I don't know what . . . I can't let it capture me!

—Go into hyperspace, Norby!

Yobo and Fargo yelled, but they seemed far away. Jeff's mind joined Norby's, tighter than ever before, and he felt that together they could escape from the force trying to control them.

"Well, at last!" Fargo said.

In the viewscreen was the gray gloom of hyperspace, and Norby's emotive circuits seemed to be calming down.

—Thanks, Jeff. Don't tell Yobo and Fargo. Wouldn't want to upset them until we find out what happened. Maybe it was my imagination.

—Can robots have imagination?

—I don't know. All I know is that whatever it was is gone now. That means that if it was real and not imaginary, it can't get into hyperspace.

"Are we headed for Earth?" Yobo asked with suspicious mildness, which meant that he knew something had gone wrong.

"Yes, sir," said Norby. "Here we are . . . oops!"

They popped out into normal space above a planet that didn't look much like Earth because it was covered with active volcanoes spouting lava over the surface.

"You've brought us to Io, Norby!" Yobo paused for a better look. "No, that's not Io. Too big, and there seems to be some water between the volcanoes and—hey! Look out!"

A large grayish object riccocheted off the protective field of

8

the ship and hurtled on down to the surface of the planet. Jeff saw that in the space near the ship there were many objects, some dark and solid, some fuzzy and gray.

"Comets! Meteorites! Where are we?" asked Fargo.

"It's when," said Norby, his half a head sunk so low in his barrel that only the tops of his eyes showed. "I seem to have miscalculated and gone back four billion years. Earth is still being bombarded by the debris left over from the formation of our solar system. Look at that big comet go in. Its water will help make an ocean."

"I did not come along on this trip to get a paleoastronomy lesson. I am not amused," Yobo said. "Norby, take us home!"

"Yes, sir." There was a lurch, another moment of gray gloom, and then Earth reappeared, this time with an ocean into which *The Hopeful* was falling.

"Norby!" Yobo shouted. "What happened to our antigrav?"

"I can't seem to control—but don't worry, we've come way up in time. And I've slowed us so we won't hit the water hard."

The ship sank just under the surface, missing a small animal with four flippers, a bulky tail, a long snaky neck, and a snaky head with beady eyes that peered through the water at the ship.

Yobo groaned. "Well, I always thought it would be fascinating to visit the Cretaceous period and see a live baby plesiosaur, which seems awfully small, but right now I want to go to Manhattan, *during my own century!*"

Norby waved an arm. "I'm sorry, everybody. I had a spot of trouble near Space Command and the effects haven't quite worn off."

"Great galaxy!" Fargo yelled. "My gorgeous blond fiancée is about one hundred million years in the future. Thanks to this mixed-up robot I'm going to be too late for my wedding."

"You mean too early," Jeff said.

2

No Time Is Safe

Norby plugged in again. The humans waited. Nothing happened except that a much larger plesiosaur joined the first.

"Mother and child, no doubt," said Yobo. "Quite at home here, which we are not. Norby . . ."

To distract the admiral, Jeff said, "They're a kind called elasmosaurus. The adults like that mother plesiosaur can grow to about twelve meters long." He touched Norby.

—Did you come to the Cretaceous period on purpose, Norby?

—Not exactly. Whatever threatened me when I was near Mars somehow made me come here. I don't know why. I can't explain.

—Please try to get us to our own time—

Jeff's telepathic communication was interrupted by the crash of a winged creature with a furry, crested head. It had dived through the ocean surface with its wickedly pointed, toothless jaw aimed at the baby elasmosaurus.

"Wow!" said Fargo. "A pteranodon! And they have hair! It was invented twice in evolution—by them and by mammals."

The mother sea reptile instantly struck at the flying one, her very toothy jaws closing around its oddly hairy neck. Blood clouded the scene from the watchers inside *The Hopeful*.

"If Norby's been struck by incompetence, I have not," Fargo announced, manipulating the controls. The ship rose above the bloodied water. "We must be over a continental shelf, because there's land over there, so we can always . . . um. Just what is that coming over the hill?"

"Tyrannosaurus rex," said Yobo. "Norby!"

"I'm trying. Maybe it would be easier to go through time if I took the ship beyond Earth's atmosphere again."

Nobody spoke while *The Hopeful* shot past the outer atmosphere and approached the Moon.

Jeff shivered. Neil Armstrong would eventually set the first human foot on that Moon. After many years, orbital space settlements and Luna City would be built, and Yobo's people would settle Mars, but right now the distant ancestors of all humans were tiny mammals scuttling out of the way of the dinosaurs.

"I'm getting a message," Norby said.

"Put it on screen," Yobo ordered.

"It's auditory only." Norby touched a switch and a strange voice filled the control room. Jeff couldn't understand a word of what was said.

"That language is not in my memory banks," Norby said. "I doubt if it's from a time traveler because I'm probably the only being in the universe capable of time travel, and it's not the language of the Others."

Jeff gulped. He trusted the Others, that ancient race of vaguely humanoid beings who—in Jeff's time—lived only in space ships and were completely peaceful.

Norby added, "The message is from a ship that's now coming around the Moon."

The alien ship was round, with spokes sticking out at what seemed to be random intervals. The spokes flashed as the ship moved across the shadowed quarter of the Moon like a swollen firefly. The flashes kept on coming, straight at *The Hopeful*.

Yobo grunted. "That ship is firing at *us*. Norby, take us out of here!"

In spite of her protective field, *The Hopeful* shuddered from the first impact and her lights flickered until the gray of hyperspace filled the viewscreen.

"We're back in our own time," Norby announced.

"Hyperspace is supposed to be dimensionless and time-less," Yobo argued, "so how can you be sure we're in our own time?"

"I don't exactly know how I time travel, or how I use hyper-space, but I know I did both at the same time, only there isn't any time in hyperspace, yet we're back in our own present, I think. . . ."

"You think!"

Fargo interrupted the admiral's anger. "Say, that alien ship could not have originated in our solar system during any time in the past or present. Therefore it must be capable of travel-ing in hyperspace. Suppose it follows us?"

"But—" Norby began.

"Of course it's followed us," Yobo said. "Didn't anyone hear the clunk of metal against our hull? And isn't anyone watching the airlock telltale light that just went on?"

"Another message," Norby said. "You will all be pleased with how competent I have become."

"What message?" Fargo roared.

Norby said, "This is our own time, because it's the ship of the Others. I'll put the message on audio."

"Permission to come aboard?" Everyone recognized the voice.

"Granted, Rembrandt," said Fargo.

The Other's real name was hard to pronounce so Jeff had called him Rembrandt because he was an artist. He was as bald as Yobo, and looked humanoid except for a third eye in his forehead and an extra pair of arms. He spoke Terran Basic with a New York accent, having learned it from Lizzie.

After Rembrandt had been told what happened, he took a deep breath and stretched his four arms as if trying to relieve tension. Ordinarily the Other wore an expression of serenity and kindness, but this time Jeff saw that although the kind-ness was still there, the serenity was not.

"My friends, it is clear that long before my own ancestors

evolved on the planet of our origin, well-advanced civilizations already existed—including one that is not friendly to any spacefaring species."

Yobo nodded. "It's upsetting to find a hostile alien race in our solar system, even if it was long ago. I only hope that they don't have time travel."

"They don't," Norby said. "Scanning them was difficult, but I'm fairly certain that they didn't have any of the metal that gives me time travel ability. Their ship's engine seemed very strange, controlled by something ring shaped, but what's even stranger, there was no capacity for hyperdrive."

"Humph!" said Yobo. "Then those aliens could not have come from beyond Earth's solar system. Yet they must have, for no such civilization arose at any time on Earth."

"Maybe it was a sleep ship, or they were robots," Jeff said.

"I don't think so," said Norby. "I didn't scan any equipment for a sleep ship."

"What were the aliens like?" Fargo asked.

"I don't know. I think they were organic, but I can't be sure. I was focused on . . ."

"On what?" asked Jeff.

"On the ring. Beautiful. Very strange . . ."

"Norby!"

At the sound of Jeff's voice, the little robot seemed to come out of a trance. "Oh. I guess we'd better get on with our important journey."

"Wait a minute, Norby," said Yobo. He turned to Rembrandt. "Were you looking for us?"

"Yes. My ship monitors transmissions from your Federation, including news items, so I learned of the forthcoming nuptials. I wanted to attend, in disguise, but Yib refused to reenter normal space near your solar system."

"Yib?" asked Fargo.

"You Immense Brain. Norby's name for the computer that runs Rembrandt's ship," Jeff said.

Norby's antenna was out. "Yib's made contact with me

telepathically. She says there's danger in the Terran solar system. Danger to artificial intelligence."

"What does that mean?" asked Yobo.

"There is no other information."

Fargo paled. "You mean we can't go out of hyperspace to attend my wedding?"

"Unlike Yib, I'm brave," Norby said. "I'll take you to Earth, Fargo."

"No, Norby," Jeff said. "It could be bad for you."

"Don't worry so much, Jeff. The danger was near Mars, not Earth. We—I—should be safe in Manhattan."

Yobo raised his eyebrows. "I hope so. Very well, Norby, take us to Earth and I'll alert Space Command to scan for intruders or any unusual computer problems."

Rembrandt rose. "I will get some supplies from my ship and then I will journey in yours . . . if you don't mind."

Fargo smiled. "I want you at my wedding, Rembrandt. We'll cover your arms with a cape, put a beret on your head to hide your third eye, and nobody will know which of my friends you are. I have a feeling that I'm going to need all the help I can get to become an authentically married man."

"Okay, everybody," Norby announced. "We're going to Earth."

Jeff shut his eyes. There was a terrific lurch, and he opened them.

3

Wedding Bells and Horns

The Hopeful was entering an atmosphere. Norby said, "You see? My genius prevails. Here's Earth, at the right time."

Fargo scowled. "You have been inefficient, Norby. Although your misadventure took only thirty minutes of our biological time, according to the ship's computer we've lost four hours Earthtime and my wedding is in an hour! Albany will be annoyed."

"I already am," Yobo said. "Time traveling is not conducive to good digestion. My breakfast, in spite of the fact that I feel I had it several years ago, is not settling well. Land gently on top of your apartment."

"You'll be all right, Admiral," Fargo said. "The wedding feast will include some of your favorite Martian delicacies. Rembrandt, will you be able to eat?"

"We have similar metabolisms and I enjoy human food."

Jeff touched Norby.

—Do you sense any of whatever it was that threatened you near Space Command?

—No. Yib must have tuned into something that's at least as far away from Earth as Mars.

—Maybe it was Garc the Great after all.

—Jeff, it's hard to believe that the kind of power I felt, and that Yib detected, could be due to a silly prankster like Garc, whoever he is.

—Well, let's be careful.

"Come on, Norby!" Fargo exclaimed. "I'm in a hurry!"

The small ship floated down to Manhattan, across Central Park and Fifth Avenue to the Wells's apartment building.

"There's Lizzie on our roof," Jeff said. "Norby, don't sit *The Hopeful* on Lizzie's new yellow chassis—it looks freshly washed and polished."

With amazing precision, Norby set the ship gently onto the roof, as far from the waiting yellow taxi as possible.

Lizzie flashed her headlights in greeting as everyone walked out of the ship's airlock. "Welcome, kind human sirs," she began, until Rembrandt emerged.

"That is, kind sirs of any species. Welcome, Rembrandt of the Others. Please, all of you must hurry. You are so late that the bride and her father are worried. Fargo, sir, your wedding clothes are at Gracie Mansion, where you must go at once."

Norby grabbed Fargo. "I'll get you there quicker."

"Not through hyperspace!" Fargo shouted as he and Norby zoomed over *The Hopeful*, heading northeast.

Jeff was miffed. While he realized that nobody else needed to dress—he was already in his best uniform, the admiral was in his best nonuniform, and Rembrandt always wore a flowing green outfit—he felt that Norby could at least have said good-bye before taking Fargo.

"It is as well," said Lizzie. "Four humanoids plus Norby would not have fitted comfortably into my cab. Please hurry, kind sirs."

"Not so fast, Lizzie," Yobo rumbled. "I know that we must be at the wedding on time since Jeff is best man and I am giving the bride away because her father is performing the ceremony. Nevertheless I insist that we take a few moments in the Wells's apartment to use the facilities and get Rembrandt a disguise. Wait for us."

As Jeff followed the admiral to the roof door, he heard Rembrandt say, "I took care of my excretory needs in my own ship, so I will wait with you, Lizzie."

She answered, "Tell me tales of the Others, sir."

"We are peaceful scientists and artists now, but I will tell you about the days long ago when we were not as civilized."

"Oh?" said Lizzie. "Were your ancestors like humans?"

* * *

The ceremony took place on the back lawn of Gracie Mansion, from which terraced gardens sloped down to the tidal estuary called the East River, slate blue in the distance. The affair was captured by holov cameras focused, fortunately, on the bridal couple and not on the guests.

Fargo's undeniably manly form, as he would have put it, was resplendent in a white bodysuit. Carrying white flowers and dressed in shimmering blue that matched her eyes, Albany was more beautiful than Jeff had ever seen her.

Suddenly Jeff noticed, almost with dismay, that Rembrandt was gazing at the bride with an expression of intense happiness. Perhaps the Other was fascinated by her loveliness merely because he was an artist.

At the beginning of the ceremony, when Leo Jones announced, "We are here to affirm an ongoing relationship," Norby embarrassed Jeff by giving a tinny laugh, but he seemed dignified enough when it was time for the exchange of rings.

Norby was the ring bearer and handed them over solemnly, but his other hand was touching Jeff.

—Rings remind me of that alien ship back in the Cretaceous. The engine . . . or the ring . . . I don't know. Something scared me.

—It's now over sixty-five million years in the past, Norby.

—I've read some of those human stories about magic rings. Have you, Jeff?

—Sure. I've read the fairy tales, the Ring operas, and Tolkien's stories. You don't think the Cretaceous aliens had magic, do you?

—No. As you humans say, things seem magical only when you don't understand how they work. I don't know why I keep thinking about the alien ship . . . hey! An odd piece of human data has just popped out of my memory circuits. A thirteenth-century pope said—I paraphrase—that the roundness of rings is to make people remember they're passing

17

through time into eternity. But you mortal humans don't need rings to remind you of that. Come to think of it, even my parts will wear out someday.

—Don't start brooding about mortality, Norby. Pay attention to the ceremony.

But Jeff himself was not paying much attention because he was remembering how King Solomon's ring was supposed to let him travel out into the universe, talk with animals, and have the power to seal up nasty demons in jars.

Well, Norby's works are sealed up in a barrel but he isn't a demon, thought Jeff. And because I've met Norby, I can talk with certain alien animals, and travel around the universe. Norby is like a magic ring. . . .

The ceremony was ending. Leo Jones smiled and said, "I now pronounce you wife and husband. Also daughter and son. Fargo, you may kiss . . . yes. Good at it, isn't he?"

Applause burst from the small audience there in person, the housekeeping robots rang little bells, and Lizzie (hovering at the edge of the garden) tooted her horn.

There was no media coverage of the reception inside the mansion, so the great public could not see how many Martian delicacies Jeff ate. Too many. He felt stuffed by the time Fargo and Albany cut the huge white-frosted peach and blueberry wedding cake in the old-fashioned dining room with its permiplast-protected 1830 wallpaper.

Eventually, Fargo led Albany to the elegant curving staircase. "Thanks, friends and family. We're going to change for our honeymoon trip to the space museum resort in Luna City. My new father-in-law is lending us Jonesy."

"Jonesy?" a guest asked.

"My private space yacht," Leo said proudly. "Take good care of her, you two."

Albany threw a white rose to Norby. "Special thanks to my ring bearer."

Catching it, Norby said to Jeff, "If I could cry, I would."

Once the newlyweds were upstairs, Jeff felt rather lost and looked for someone he knew to talk to, but Leo and his second wife, Hedy, were deep in a discussion of Federation politics with Admiral Yobo and Hedy's mother, Merlina, the soap opera star, while Hedy's brother Horace finished the rest of the cake.

Norby was nearby, but he was busy playing with the holov set, finding his favorite show, the ancient one about a starship named *Enterprise*.

Rembrandt walked over to Jeff. "You seem sad. Are not weddings supposed to be happy occasions?"

"Sure, but Fargo seems so much more grown up now. I mean, he always was, being ten years older, but now . . ."

"He's a married man."

"Yes. I guess I'll go out back and talk to Lizzie. She must be lonely."

Rembrandt smiled, as if he knew that Jeff was feeling even lonelier.

"May I go with you?" Rembrandt asked. "Lizzie is an interesting mechanism—self-aware like my Yib, but with more personality. Like you, Norby," he added when Norby's back eyes popped open and the robot began to make a grinding sound.

"Lizzie's all right," Norby said, "but without talents like mine. I'll join you later."

"Okay," Jeff said listlessly.

"I mean now. I'd rather be with you, Jeff."

Feeling much better, Jeff led Rembrandt and Norby out the back door in time to see the sunset reflected as a gold sheen on the white buildings across the East River.

"On a planet like Earth, day's end can be so beautiful."

"Yes, Rembrandt," said Jeff, "I guess this day is ending well even if it didn't start out that way, with us floundering around in the distant past."

"My fault," Norby said softly. He hadn't admitted as much

to Yobo and Fargo, but there was something about Rembrandt that made people want to tell the truth. "I felt drawn to the Cretaceous, and I don't know why."

Rembrandt's eyes widened. "I have studied the history of your planet, and know that that era was a turning point. I do not recommend returning to it. Is it not possible to make mistakes while time traveling, thus changing history, and perhaps creating difficulties in restoring the rightful past?"

"Yes," Jeff and Norby answered simultaneously. They looked at each other and fell silent.

"Ah, well," Rembrandt said, "the important thing right now is that the young couple is happily united. I am delighted that I could attend such a charming ceremony here. The more I see of Earth, the more I like it."

At that moment, a fleet of air taxis flew overhead and began hovering over the mansion. Jeff could hear the other guests leaving the mansion by the front door.

Norby's antenna suddenly shot out and his back eyes shut.

"Norby, is something wrong?" Jeff asked.

"I think the wedding publicity must have given someone a clue. I sense . . . an arrival."

Before Jeff had time to wonder what Norby meant, Jonesy flew out of the mayor's attached garage, circled around, and returned to land on the back lawn. Albany ran from the airlock.

"Forgot our Oola!" She dashed into the house.

Fargo grinned from the airlock. "It wouldn't do to leave Oola with my father-in-law much longer. She does have a tendency to overeat salads and get sick all over the mansion rugs."

Albany returned, holding an irate All-Purpose-Pet in her arms. Oola had been bioengineered on another planet, was vegetarian, and could change her shape to whatever pet you happened to be thinking about. Right now she was a cat, and her green fur was standing on end.

Oola's not just annoyed, thought Jeff. She's scared. Of being left behind? Or of something else?

Then he noticed that Lizzie had retreated to the edge of the lawn. Her headlight covers drooped, as if she were disappointed at not being able to take the newlyweds on their honeymoon trip.

Jeff walked over to Lizzie to cheer her up when suddenly her horn blared.

"Look out!" Lizzie cried, sounding terrified. "Look up!"

The other taxis were forming a circle directly over the backyard while, on the other side of the mansion, their would-be fares were yelling, "Taxi! Taxi!"

It looked to Jeff as if someone was already in one of the taxis. He was trying to get a better glimpse when he heard Norby call out.

"Help!" Norby's head, arms, and legs retracted into his body, then he fell to the ground with a thump.

Before Jeff could reach Norby, the silvery barrel rose in the air sideways, not as if Norby had turned on his antigrav, but as if he were being drawn by a tractor beam.

Jeff leapt to grab him but it was too late. Norby was pulled straight into the circle of taxis.

"Go into hyperspace, Norby!"

There was no answer. The taxis closed around the robot until Jeff could see only a glint of Norby's silvery barrel inside the strange cage.

Lizzie said, "Somebody is controlling those taxis and stealing Norby!"

"I'll get him," Fargo said from Jonesy's loudspeaker as the small space yacht moved toward the taxis.

"Come back for me," Albany yelled, shoving Oola into Jeff's arms and using her wrist band to summon police aircars.

Fargo did not return. The assembled taxis closed ranks around Jonesy, too.

Rembrandt and Jeff could only gaze upward as helplessly as everyone else.

"What sort of power can do that?" asked Rembrandt.

"Connection," said Lizzie.

"What are you talking about, Lizzie?" Jeff said angrily, furious with himself for not paying attention to Norby's warning. Oola was hissing and squirming, so Jeff stuffed her under the front of his tunic.

"I cannot explain, Jeff sir, except to say that it is a power to connect machines with each other, and force us to do what we're told. So far, I can resist this power, perhaps because I am different from the other taxis."

"So is Norby."

Lizzie had no answer to that.

Admiral Yobo came out the back door. "What is going on?"

"Renegade taxis, sir Admiral," Lizzie said. "They've stolen Norby and Fargo!"

Albany said, "Lizzie, if you're not affected, I'm commandeering you as a pursuit vehicle." She plunged into Lizzie's backseat, followed quickly by Rembrandt.

Lizzie flew toward the other taxis before Jeff had a chance to get inside, so he yelled, "Wait for me, Albany—I want to go with you!"

But Lizzie was already out of reach.

4

Collaring a Talent

The admiral, Leo Jones, and Jeff were alone in the backyard, for everyone else was out front, shouting for taxis.

Jeff tried not to look as anxious as he felt. Two beings he loved were unaccountably out of contact. Although Fargo had access to Jonesy's loudspeaker, there had been no word since the space yacht had been drawn inside the cage of taxis.

And Norby should have been yelling to Jeff, out loud and telepathically. But there was nothing. Did the cage of taxis prevent communication outside it? Or—Jeff shuddered—had Norby been deactivated?

Lit by the floodlights from Gracie Mansion, Lizzie hovered directly over the cage, which could not move up without hitting her. When the cage tried to move to the side, not only did Lizzie follow, but the way was eventually blocked by the trees around the yard and by the mansion's roof.

"My daughter is using Lizzie as a police chase vehicle," Leo Jones said proudly. "She and your friend Rembrandt will get Fargo and Norby out of the clutches of whatever villain is controlling the taxis."

Through Lizzie's loudspeaker, Albany shouted, "Thief, this is Lieutenant Albany Jones of the Manhattan Police Force. Release my ship and the robot you have stolen or I will be forced to fire."

"Can Albany's gun deactivate the computers in all those taxis?" Jeff whispered.

Leo shook his head. "I don't think so, but it doesn't matter since my daughter is only pretending to have a gun. She told me she wasn't taking it with her on the trip."

"Release your prisoners!"

A scratchy tenor voice answered Albany from one of the other taxis. "Go away, police person. I will not release the robot and that small, fast starship. Their brains are needed. If you don't go away I will be forced to do something nasty."

"My husband, Fargo Wells, is in that ship you've stolen!"

"That's not my fault. He'll just have to come along for the ride. He will be released eventually—or maybe not, if you don't leave me alone to do my job."

"What is your job?"

The voice did not answer.

"I demand that you release my husband *now* and also the robot, who belongs to his brother, Jeff Wells."

"The robot must remain in my possession. Try to accept the fact that I am very powerful and you cannot defeat me."

"The inevitable overinflated ego of a villain," Yobo muttered, his burly arms folded across his massive chest.

"I heard that," said the hoarse voice. "I am not a villain. I am a genius, going on an important mission. Get out of my way or that taxi will be smashed."

The hovering cage moved up until the top taxi bumped against Lizzie. Her door opened and Albany started to climb out and down to the cage.

"No, Albany!" Yobo yelled. "Stay where you are until your fellow police arrive. If you try to get down to Fargo you'll be trapped like him. He must be unable to work the ship's controls or he'd have communicated with us by now."

Leo Jones called out, "Please, Albany! Be careful."

"I must get to Fargo. He may be unconscious!"

Nobody added—or dead.

"Here come the police aircars," Leo said with relief.

Ten large squad cars positioned themselves in the air around Lizzie, looking down at the cage of taxis.

Leo whispered, "The flying police can stun people in aircars, and turn off the engines if necessary. They won't aim at Lizzie, but I'm worried about Fargo."

"Tell them not to fire," Yobo said. "It's too dangerous."

"I—wait. Albany's back inside Lizzie and is no doubt communicating by intercom with the rest of the police."

"All taxis must descend or we will shoot," the police radio boomed out. "Scanning shows that the thief is in a late-model exploration space suit. Who are you?"

No one answered.

A short blast from one of the squad cars rocked the cage of taxis. "That's a warning. Descend, thief."

"I won't. You are being foolish."

"Who are you, thief?" Yobo yelled. "If you're powerful and doing something important, you should not be afraid to reveal your identity."

"Very well, attend! I am Garc the Great! That is all you have to know."

"Garc the graffiti artist," Jeff said.

"Yes, I am good at that, too."

The police radio said, "A tie-in to Computer Prime reveals that no Garc is listed as a Federation citizen. The name must be a pseudonym. What is your real name, thief?"

"Won't tell. Go away. I'm busy making connections."

The police radio continued. "Descend, or you may be injured when your vehicle falls. Your space suit will not save you from harm when you crash. Give yourself up to custody."

Jeff gasped. "But Jonesy will fall along with the renegade taxis. Fargo might be injured. And Norby will fall. . . ."

Leo whispered, "The police are only threatening."

"Naughty police," said Garc. "You can't make me descend, because I have more power than you. I can control the computers in your vehicles, and I can destroy you. You are wrong to try stopping Garc the Great. My mission will harm nobody. I am doing only good. Leave me alone."

"Kidnapping my husband and the robot Norby is doing harm," said Albany. "How can this mission of yours be good?"

"I am creating new life, connecting what should be connected. Go away because I must leave now. If you don't, I will not be responsible for the consequences to all of you."

Jeff felt as if time had stopped, for none of the vehicles in the air moved and no one spoke. The people wanting taxis had stopped yelling.

The silence was broken by a screeching growl. "Wowrrrr!"

"Stop that, Oola. You're scratching me." She was trying to climb up inside Jeff's tunic to reach his shoulder, which her small mind apparently thought was closer to where she wanted to go.

Jeff pulled her out and put her on his shoulder, saying, "Settle down. You can't get to Albany and Fargo that way."

"What's the matter, Cadet? You look thunderstruck."

"Admiral! I do have a way of getting to Norby. You're very strong—could you manage to let me stand on your shoulders?"

"Jeff, you can hardly reach Lizzie that way. I know you're very worried about your brother and your robot, but you'd better let the police handle this."

"I don't think they can, sir. If I could get closer to Norby, I might be able to communicate with him and break the paralyzing spell, or whatever it is that Garc's doing to artificial brains."

"I understand your wish, Jeff, but what good will it do to be only a little higher up?"

"Well, I don't think I could easily climb any of those trees and I don't want to go inside and up to the roof, and . . ."

"What is your point, Cadet?"

"Admiral, hurry—lift me up to stand on your shoulders. Then I'll jump off."

"What!"

"I'd forgotten that Oola's collar—the one Fargo and I got from the dragons of Jamya—has antigrav like the aircars, only miniature."

"That collar is much too small for you, Jeff," Yobo said,

26

"and it's activated only by the wearer, who is a not very intelligent pet. If Oola doesn't activate the collar's antigrav in time, both of you will fall."

"I probably won't break anything, sir. It's worth trying."

"Very well. If you fall, I'll endeavor to catch you before you reach the ground." Yobo helped Jeff onto his broad shoulders and then—puffing a little—stood upright, holding Jeff's legs to steady him.

"Oola! Up! Up!" shouted Jeff, trying to balance himself on Yobo's shoulders. He pictured in his mind a small animal falling but saving herself by soaring upward.

"Cadet, as time passes, you are not getting lighter and I am not as young as I used to be."

"I'm counting on the fact that Oola hates falling."

"At the moment Oola is a cat and could easily jump out of your arms to land the way cats do, right side up and on their feet. Hold tightly to her collar so she can't jump off you. It may also impress her with the fact that she has to take you with her if she activates the antigrav."

"Okay. Got it, sir."

Oola was squirming, and when Jeff tried to stroke her, she snarled. "Oola, if you're determined to get to Albany and Fargo, go *up!*"

Admiral Yobo was puffing harder. "You know that creature is not bright enough to understand what you're saying."

"Yowrrr!" Oola batted Jeff in the face, as if the whole thing were his fault.

"Bad cat!" Suddenly Jeff remembered that Oola did understand a few crucial words. "Go *up*, Oola, or *no salad*."

Oola stopped squirming. "Worw?"

"Good girl. We'll go to Albany."

She consented to be held in Jeff's arms. He gripped her collar carefully.

"I'm going to jump, Admiral."

"Jeff . . ."

"Here goes." As he jumped off the Admiral's shoulders,

Jeff again thought "up" and pictured in his mind a small green animal yowling in front of an empty food dish.

Oola went up—but not slowly, the way one should using an alien antigrav collar. She acted as if she'd just remembered the collar's potential and was determined to take full advantage. With Jeff holding onto her and her collar, they sped toward the cage of taxis around Norby and Fargo.

"Good luck!" Yobo shouted.

5

Vanishing Villain

Oola would not slow down enough for Jeff to get more than a glimpse at the renegade taxis, but inside one there was indeed a figure in a space suit. As Jeff sailed by, Garc saw him and lifted a large circular object. It looked like a golden ring, its outer surface carved with a jagged pattern like strokes of lightning.

"Stop, Oola."

Oola paid no attention. She sped up and over the cage of taxis because they were too close together around Jonesy for her to be able to reach Fargo, upon whom she doted.

"Oola, go back."

But Oola adored Albany, too, so she landed with a thump—of Jeff—on Lizzie's roof.

The roof's sliding panel promptly opened. When Jeff and the All-Purpose-Pet fell into Lizzie, Oola plastered herself to Albany and—apparently confused about which animal shape she was in—whined like an unhappy puppy.

Jeff picked himself off poor Rembrandt, who moved closer to Albany so Jeff could squeeze next to Lizzie's door.

"Now what?" Albany asked. "Looks like stalemate. I've ordered the police not to shoot, because Fargo could be hurt."

Garc the Great apparently had other ideas. The mass of taxis moved up, taking Jonesy and Norby with them and pushing Lizzie as if she were weightless. The police squad cars followed helplessly.

Rembrandt said, "I must remind you that since Garc is in a space suit, he can take his taxis beyond your atmosphere if he chooses."

"In space, Jonesy will protect Fargo whether he's unconscious or not," Albany said. "But I don't know about us. Lizzie, how high can you go and how protected are you?"

"I am able to travel above the atmosphere, Lieutenant sir, for I am shielded against the stresses of space. But I am duty bound to warn you that I do not have a supply of oxygen, and once I am sealed against space, the air in my interior will not last long. Taxis are prohibited from carrying anything that would make it possible for someone using them to escape into space."

"Unless the passenger had a space suit equipped with an oxygen supply," Jeff said. "Which Garc probably has."

"Blast," said Albany.

"We're rising again," Rembrandt said. "Lizzie, how is it that you are not affected by Garc's control of computer brains?"

"I do not know, sir Other. Norby is much more powerful and intelligent than I. Fargo's ship, Jonesy, is run by a computer bigger than mine, although it has no more self-awareness than the usual taxi. Yet these stronger computers have been taken, while I can still resist the Connector's pull."

"Norby's self-aware, too, yet he's been taken." Jeff said.

"It's the Connector ring," Lizzie said sadly. "It is a dangerously powerful object. I do not know how I know this—oh, I think I do know now. I have examined my memory banks, and I feel . . . I am sorry to be imprecise, and I realize that robots are not supposed to have intuition, but nevertheless, I *feel* as if I have somehow received that information from Norby."

"He's alive!" Jeff exclaimed.

"Oh, yes, Jeff Wells sir. Alive, and conscious, but unable to function."

"Except telepathically. Perhaps I can reach him that way." Jeff closed his eyes and thought hard.

"Anything?" Albany asked impatiently.

"No," Jeff said sadly. "I couldn't even 'feel' him the way Lizzie does."

Another, bigger police aircar arrived. "Lieutenant Jones! This is your commanding officer, Captain O'Neil."

"Sir?" Albany said into her intercom.

"Jones, I am countermanding your order against opening fire. We must ground this Garc."

"Wait!" Albany shouted.

The police cars all fired at once, avoiding Lizzie.

At first, nothing seemed to happen. Suddenly Lizzie vibrated as the police cars were hurled from the cage of taxis like leaves blown away from an airjet. They did not fall, however, and after righting themselves, they began to fly back toward Lizzie and the cage.

"You see how dangerous it is to mess with me! I am Garc the Great and I can toss you away again. Now I must do my work. Good-bye, New Yorkers. I never did like your city."

Lizzie lurched as if struck, and suddenly the view of Gracie Mansion disappeared. Jeff's ears popped, he felt blinded, and for a moment he feared that a bomb had gone off. In the midst of the confusion, he thought he heard somebody say something important, but he could not make out what it was.

Lizzie's internal lights came on. "Are you intact, sirs?"

"I'm intact," Rembrandt said. "How are the two of you?"

"Okay," Jeff said. "Stop that, Oola." She was yowling and trying to burrow into Albany's armpit.

"We are in hyperspace," Rembrandt said calmly. "The cage of taxis probably moved here and carried Lizzie with them. My limited scanning abilities indicate that the hyperdrive Garc used was unlike my Yib's, so it is probable that he made Norby accomplish the transition to hyperspace."

Jeff said, "Maybe it wasn't Norby but Garc's strange ring device. Maybe it contains the same alien metal that's in Norby."

"No. We Others can detect the rare alien metal built into

31

Norby, giving him his extraordinary abilities. Our hyperspace engines, and those of other species, do not contain this metal, and I did not detect any such metal near Garc."

Albany bit her lip. "If Garc is using Norby's talents, then he could have disappeared into time as well as hyperspace."

Jeff sighed. "And without Norby, there's no way we can follow the other taxis through time, but perhaps Garc is nearby in hyperspace."

Rembrandt said, "I have some telepathic ability, and I do not sense that he is anywhere near us. Perhaps you could find out by using your hycom. Do you have this, Lizzie?"

"Yes, sir Other, but it does not seem to work in hyperspace. I am trying without success to notify Mayor Jones of our whereabouts, and I cannot make contact with Garc's taxi."

Albany sighed. "Unlike Norby's hycom, the one invented by the Federation has to start from and end in normal space, so without Norby we not only have no hyperdrive or time travel but also no communication. We're trapped in hyperspace."

"Kind passengers, remember that my air supply is limited. Please calm yourselves and breathe as lightly as possible."

Oola was already panting, although it might have been due more to anxiety than to lack of oxygen. She licked Albany's chin.

One of Rembrandt's upper hands stroked Oola, and Jeff wondered if he wanted to stroke Albany as well. Then Jeff saw that Rembrandt had shut his third eye.

After a few seconds, the Other spoke. "Do not worry, my Terran friends. We will not suffocate. I have made mind contact with my ship, which is nearby in hyperspace."

"Sir Other, will I have to stay outside your ship, alone in this awful gray nothingness?"

"No, Lizzie. There will be plenty of room for you."

She tooted her horn. "Kind sirs, I know that my horn makes no outward sound in hyperspace, but the ship of the Others

32

has just touched me and I felt I should acknowledge the contact."

"I have instructed Yib to open the main airlock for you to enter my ship. It is ready now. Go in, Lizzie, and follow the main corridor to the stern."

The small Manhattan taxi floated on her own antigrav through the airlock and down a wide corridor to the immense observation room of Rembrandt's ship, where she opened her doors to let out her passengers. "You can breathe easily now, kind sirs. This ship has good air and efficient artificial gravity."

The two humans, one humanoid, and one All-Purpose-Pet scrambled out of Lizzie and stretched to remove the kinks caused by sitting so long in such tension.

"Welcome to my ship," Rembrandt said with a touch of pride.

Albany looked stunned, but Jeff, having been there before, felt at home with the curved lines of the room, its soft tones, and the crystal-and-light sculpture by Rembrandt. He shivered a little because the huge window at the stern was blank. There was nothing outside but hyperspace.

Where Norby and Fargo are lost, Jeff thought.

Legs and Connections

Jeff said sadly, "I've never been in your ship without Norby, Rembrandt. I wish . . . gosh!"

"What's the matter, Jeff?" Albany asked.

"Back when we were going into hyperspace, I thought I heard somebody say something important. Did any of you speak then?"

Albany frowned. "Rembrandt, Lizzie, and I said nothing when we were shoved into hyperspace, but Oola was cater-wauling. Was that what you heard?"

Jeff shook his head, trying to remember. "No, it was—blast! I've lost it."

He felt something rub against his leg. It was Oola, looking up at him and warbling. "That's the beginning of her 'I'm hungry' noise, which will soon progress to a loud wail."

Rembrandt's lower right hand reached down to pat Oola, who began nuzzling the Other's leg. "Salad is on its way for your pet. The rest of us should also eat while we decide what to do."

"I don't think I can eat much," Albany said. "As it is, my wedding feast feels as if it might come up at any moment."

"I will provide a soothing drink to take care of that prob-lem." At one gesture from Rembrandt, the floor promptly ex-truded a small table and three padded seats with backs, while a little servorobot trundled in bearing a tray of food.

A bowl of greenery was put on the floor for Oola, who pro-ceeded to chomp away with her usual enthusiasm. Jeff wished he could forget his troubles as easily as Oola forgot hers.

Lizzie plugged in to one of the room's electronic outlets and blinked her headlights. "Ah, your ship's energy feels good, Rembrandt sir. It replenishes my strength."

Jeff felt he could do with some replenishing too, so he ate one of the blue cakes that he knew tasted like almond paste.

Albany swallowed some pink liquid, raised an eyebrow, and said, "That helped. But I must find Fargo as soon as possible. Can't Yib locate Garc?"

"Yib is now reporting to me." Rembrandt paused. "I'm sorry. Yib says the vehicles that entered hyperspace with Lizzie have left it for normal space, but not near their previous location. Scanning all of normal space for them may prove to be very difficult. Do you know approximately where they could be?"

"No, especially if Garc has forced Norby to take him somewhere in time," Jeff said, trying not to cry because his two favorite beings were missing. "I can't . . . oh! Oh!"

"You look like you've remembered something," Albany said.

"Yes. When we jumped into hyperspace I must have received a telepathic message from Norby, but it wasn't in words. I think he was trying to disguise his message in case Garc could listen in. I can't think of any other reason why he'd send a picture of a round, flat animal walking along on jointed legs."

Rembrandt looked puzzled. "Perhaps it was an image you picked up from Garc himself. Something amusing he was thinking about."

"I don't think so, because it wasn't funny at all. There was something terribly sinister about the image, and . . . yes, I'm sure I sensed a feeling of desperation. Not from the walking animal, but about it. As if there were terrible danger."

"Why was this image walking, I wonder?" Rembrandt mused. "Were the animal's legs jointed like mine, or like Oola's here?"

"Neither. Terran mammals like Oola or humans have legs with softer flesh covering the harder structure of bones, and so do you, although your legs have an extra joint. The legs in the picture had a hard outer surface."

"Like robots," Albany said.

"No, it wasn't a robot. At least I don't think so, because Federation walking robots aren't jointed like that, and Norby certainly isn't."

"Then insects," Albany said, "or lobsters. Any member of Phylum Arthropoda. Three quarters of the animals on Earth belong to it. How many legs were there, Jeff?"

He closed his eyes and tried to see the image again in his mind, while everyone kept silent except Oola, purring as she ate. "I think the animal had eight legs."

Albany said, "Well, it's not an octopus—that's Phylum Mollusca—because their legs aren't jointed or hard. Insects have three pairs of legs, so if the image is meant to represent a Terran creature, it has to be one with four pairs of walking legs, and that's the arachnids, which includes scorpions. Was Norby pointing out that Garc is as dangerous as a scorpion? We already know that."

"What does the word *arachnid* mean?" asked Rembrandt.

"It's from an ancient Earth language called Greek," Jeff said. "The Greeks had a legend about a woman named Arachne who was punished for thinking she could beat the goddess Athena in a weaving contest. The Greek gods turned her into . . ."

"Jeff?" Albany's eyes widened. "Jeff, are you thinking what I'm thinking?"

"Please explain," Rembrandt said.

Jeff tried to be calm. "Rembrandt, please tell Yib to take your ship to where we can get out into normal space near Computer Prime's asteroid, between Mars and Jupiter in our solar system."

"I am doing so." After a moment the Other opened his third eye. "Can this Computer Prime tell us where Garc has gone?"

"I hope so," Albany said. "If Garc's taxis are anywhere in

our solar system, Computer Prime should be able to track them. It's the central storage and switching center for all the other computers and robots in our Federation."

Rembrandt rubbed his bald head with an upper hand and said, "We have no central computer entity, for each of our ships has an artificial brain like Yib, able to communicate telepathically with the rest of the ships and with us Others. Is your Computer Prime like that?"

Albany and Jeff both began to talk at once, but Albany stopped and said, "Your turn, Jeff."

"Norby's the only telepathic computer in the Federation, sir. And Computer Prime isn't a self-aware entity like Yib, or Norby or Lizzie. It's just a huge, well-shielded computer built in space. Its primary function is to hold and correlate the data from all the Solarweb computers."

"Which is where the arachnid comes in," Albany added.

"I still do not understand," Rembrandt said.

Jeff cleared his throat nervously, hoping he could remember what he'd learned in his Academy history courses. "After Terran computers were developed in our late twentieth century, they were soon linked into many networks. The networks were eventually joined and correlated by something called the World Wide Web, which had no central supercomputer controlling it. Lots of people used the Web but few understood it."

"Why not?" asked Rembrandt.

"Back then humans had no common language. Even their computers had mathematical languages of their own, and worked on principles that were difficult to understand."

"How strange," Rembrandt said.

Jeff nodded. "By the time humans colonized our solar system, we used Terran Basic, built largely from English because that had dominated the Web. By then, computers had microbubble brains and were intelligent enough to use the same Terran Basic, and the World Wide Web had expanded into the Solarweb."

"And the Solarweb still exists?"

"It's the linkage of all the computers, whether through optic fiber cables, satellite beams, or hycom, but most people don't use the term Solarweb because they're used to thinking of Computer Prime, the central data bank that was eventually built to monitor, correlate, and control the Solarweb."

"And that's wrong," Albany said. "If anything happened to Computer Prime, the data would still be available from the Solarweb, although it would take longer to locate and download information, which is where spiders . . ."

She paused, gazing down. "Oola, you're beginning to burp. If you eat any more it won't stay down." She gave Oola's not-quite-empty salad dish to the servorobot.

Fortunately Oola did not object, but ambled over to Lizzie, jumped inside, and went to sleep on the backseat. Lizzie herself unplugged from the connection to Yib's power source and rolled to be nearer to the humanoids.

"Spiders spin webs," Lizzie said, taking up the conversation. "The cleaning robots have to be sure to get rid of them in us taxis because customers object, although I've always thought a large spiderweb across my rear window would be decorative."

In spite of his anxiety, Jeff almost laughed because Rembrandt was looking more and more puzzled.

"Lizzie's talking about *organic* spiders," Jeff said, "but Albany and I are talking about computer programs. Norby must have been afraid that Garc could monitor a telepathic message to me, so instead of spelling the danger out, he disguised it as a picture of a ring-shaped object with spider legs."

"I do not understand," Rembrandt said.

"I think Norby was trying to give me a clue about Garc. In the early days of the World Wide Web, people sometimes used the term *spider* for a cyberspace search method, but gradually—with modern computer brains—such methods became unnecessary."

Rembrandt nodded. "And spiders travel along the cyberspace of the Solarweb?"

Jeff realized he'd trusted too much that Norby would understand and manage computer problems. "Uh, organic spiders do travel on webs, but . . ."

"The point is that spiders mainly construct webs," Lizzie said, her voice tinny with anxiety. "I told you that Garc has the Connector. It's round, and that's what Norby must have meant in the image he sent to you, Jeff."

"A connector with spider legs," Rembrandt said softly, as if trying to put the ideas together.

Lizzie did it for him. "Garc must be using the Connector to make a special web of his own to control the Federation's computer system. Such a web would control the Federation itself. I'm only a Manhattan taxi, but I still belong to the Federation computer system, and I disapprove of Garc's mischief, kind sirs. Please do something about it."

39

7

Problems with Others

In the quiet of the great room Albany and Rembrandt seemed to be thinking hard about what Lizzie said, but Jeff felt as if the hyperspace outside the ship had emptied his brain and filled it with anxiety. He knew he had to reason out the problem, but all he came up with was, "If Norby's been taken apart and his brain used . . ." Then he had to stop so he wouldn't cry.

Rembrandt said, "Since Garc made Norby work for him without taking him apart, your robot could be still intact."

Albany put down a half-eaten purple cake and stood up, clenching her fists. "I've been sitting here chatting and eating because I thought Fargo would be safe as long as he was in Jonesy, but he's not safe, not if the image Jeff got from Norby is accurate, and Lizzie's interpretation is correct. Fargo is trapped in Dad's Jonesy with no control over the computer. If the life-support systems fail, he'll die. We must rescue him!"

"They probably won't fail," Jeff said, hoping he was right. "I think that a spaceship's life support is supposed to function automatically no matter what happens to the computer."

"We can't know for certain what Garc's capable of doing."

"Does Fargo's ship contain space suits?" Rembrandt asked.

"Yes," Albany said, "but what if Garc's connector device locks in the power of control over everything? What if Fargo can't open the space suit lockers?"

"He'll use a gun to dissolve the door," Jeff said.

"There are no guns in Jonesy." Albany began to pace with an angry energy. "Rembrandt, you must take the risk of your ship being seen by Federation humans. We must go into normal space at once to rescue Fargo—and warn Computer Prime about Garc."

"We have already arrived at the hyperspace coordinates for Computer Prime," Rembrandt said, "but we cannot enter normal space. It is not merely the risk of being seen. Yib says that Garc has already arrived there and in normal space this ship will be in danger from the Connector. I am sorry, but my ship must remain in hyperspace."

"But Rembrandt, you control Yib!" Albany persisted. "You can decide to take the risk!" Jeff saw that she'd produced a stun gun from the recesses of her traveling outfit.

"Your father said you weren't carrying a gun."

"Jeff, my father wanted me to stop being a cop at least on my honeymoon, so I let him think I'd left my gun in Gracie Mansion. But I carry it because I *am* a cop. That's what I do. And now, Mr. Other, you'd better order your ship to take us into normal space—and to my husband."

Rembrandt rose to face Albany's gun. "Albany, remember that Lizzie can ward off Garc's control, so she is relatively safe in normal space, to which my ship can propel her. My technicians will fit an apparatus into her trunk that will permit Lizzie's passengers to continue breathing and to survive longer in space."

"Just how long will that take?" Albany demanded.

Rembrandt's third eye shut for a second. "Approximately two hours, during which I strongly advise that you and Jeff rest. You have each had a long day, it is now the middle of your night, and you are both tired. You will need energy for the tasks ahead of you."

"No! I won't rest!" Albany aimed the gun at Rembrandt. "I won't wait for Lizzie. Give me one of your space suits."

"That will be done in any case," Rembrandt said calmly. "The remodeling will be simple, and two suits will be ready for you and Jeff by the time the machinery is inserted in Lizzie."

"Give me a suit now, dammit! No—give me two suits now, because in two hours Fargo could be out of air!"

Jeff didn't see Rembrandt move at all, but he must have given an order, for doors opened and armed Others entered, standing behind Rembrandt.

"It's no use, Albany," Jeff said. "I almost agree with you, but Rembrandt's right—we'd be better off going in Lizzie. Even if the air in Jonesy isn't renewed, what's there will probably last many hours. And Albany, you know that Fargo can manage in most dangerous situations."

"If! Probably! We've wasted enough time already. I want to go to Fargo."

Rembrandt walked up close to Albany, his face full of compassion and—Jeff was sure—something else.

Her gun did not waver. "You may have called out your troops, Rembrandt, but I'm willing to stun all of you. Are you such a loveless people that you can't understand my love for my husband, and that I must leave *now*?"

One of Rembrandt's upper arms lightly touched her shoulder and the other touched her silky blond hair. With something like a moan, Albany began to lean toward him.

"Rembrandt . . . I won't . . ."

"Sleep, Albany. Sleep, my dear one."

She dropped the gun and collapsed, caught by all four of Rembrandt's arms.

Jeff picked up the gun and pointed it at the Other. The Others in the background moved a step forward. "Rembrandt, what did you do to her? Tell me, or I'll . . . I'll . . ."

"No need for threats, young Jefferson Wells. I have put her to sleep, and now you must sleep too."

"Get away from me! I thought you were my friend!"

A soft couch billowed up from the floor and Rembrandt tenderly placed Albany upon it. Another couch appeared.

"Your bed, Jeff. I will not put you to sleep, but if you cannot rest, a servorobot will bring a mild potion to provide your body with a short sleep."

"Short?"

"I will wake you when preparations for the journey to normal space are complete. Give me the gun, Jeff. I will return it to Albany when she wakes."

Reluctantly, Jeff handed it over.

"Come with me, Lizzie. You do not object, do you?"

"Not at all, kind Other. I am happy to become more useful to my human compatriots. But please hurry. I once read—unlike other taxis I read while waiting for fares—that time is of the essence. Although I do not understand this, perhaps you can."

"Indeed," said Rembrandt, disappearing out the door with Lizzie in his wake.

Jeff waited to see if the rest of the Others would remain to guard him, but they left as well. He remembered that Oola was inside Lizzie, so he and Albany were all the Terrans left in the great room of the Others.

He tried each door but they did not respond to his touch or to his spoken command. He was locked in.

"Rembrandt!"

No one answered.

"Yib! You must be able to hear me because you're part of this ship. I'm speaking the language of the Others, so you ought to understand me. . . . Uh, sorry. I forgot that you're telepathic. When Norby and I talk telepathically it's easier when we're touching."

He looked for anything that would remind him of the usual computer display panel in a Federation ship, but there was nothing. Angrily, he slammed his hand against the wall, and caught a feeling of amusement.

He kept his hand there.

—I didn't know you had emotive circuits, Yib.

—I do. The Others do not realize it, but Norby knows, and you are apparently able to sense them.

—You can stifle your emotive circuits, Yib, because this predicament—Norby's and Fargo's—isn't funny.

—That is correct. I was merely amused at your violent way of making contact with the ship.

—If you understand the danger to Norby and Fargo, please rush things along.

—I am, but remember that I must protect myself.

—That's selfish.

—Is it not one of the Federation laws of robotics that a robot must not allow a sentient organic being to come to harm?

—Well, sort of. But maybe you apply that only to protecting the Others in your ship, while in doing so you may allow harm to come to . . .

—I would protect Norby and Lizzie and you organic beings from the Federation just as much as I protect my permanent residents. You are being illogical, Jefferson Wells. You have no hard evidence that Norby and Fargo have been harmed so far, or will be seriously harmed in the future.

—Can't you just try going into normal space near Garc and finding out if it's dangerous for a computer brain that's so different from anything in the Federation?

—Norby is different, and he was taken.

Jeff removed his hand from the wall. She has me there, he thought. I can't ask Rembrandt or Yib to endanger themselves. And this ship is a floating library and museum of artworks made and collected by the Others for millennia. It cannot be consigned to Garc.

—Good reasoning, Jefferson Wells.

—How am I hearing your thoughts, Yib?

There was again a ripple of amusement.

—Through the floor.

—Do you hear what everyone on the ship says?

—Yes.

—Do you also know what everyone on the ship is thinking?

—Yes.

—Is Rembrandt in love with Albany?

—I do not answer questions about private thoughts.

—Is there any way of turning off your telepathy, so people in a room will not be spied on?

—I am not a spy. I perform my function.

—Answer the question, Yib. Can you be turned off here?

—Yes. Just ask.

She sounded very hurt, but before he could change his mind, Jeff said, aloud, "Stop all telepathic and audio listening in this room. Please."

—I comply. I hope you will sleep, Jefferson Wells. Good-bye until you ask to have me return.

Jeff was sure it was done, and he almost laughed at himself, for he felt lonely. He walked over to Albany's couch and gazed at her.

She's so beautiful and intelligent and brave. I don't blame Rembrandt. I must get Fargo back.

With Yib gone and the doors still locked (he tried them) there was nothing else to do, so he got on the second couch and had unpleasant thoughts.

I can't sleep. Fargo's in danger. Norby needs me. I can't control what's happening. I can't sleep. . . .

He gritted his teeth and almost wished he had not sent Yib away. Finally, he tried to relax by whispering a version of his solstice litany.

"I am part of the life of the Terran solar system, which is also part of the whole Universe. . . ."

He stopped because his tired mind was churning so hard that he felt muddled up. He took a deep breath, let it out slowly, and went on.

". . . so there is nothing really alien. Even Garc. Or Rembrandt. Or Yib. Maybe Computer Prime has always been alive, too, so whatever Garc can do it will be part of its life and maybe all us living things can cope. . . ."

This is not going well, he thought.

But what I said is true, isn't it? Norby and Lizzie and Yib are as alive as any organic being. Norby's a genius at coping.

45

He makes mistakes, of course, because he's got alien and Terran computer parts mixed up, but that's all right. . . .

Coping. Norby would try to cope no matter what sort of pickle he was in.

Jeff took another deep breath, let it out, and began again.

"I am part of the living Universe, which is One. All of us one with all parts, so I will respect all life, organic or not. Whatever's happening to him, Norby knows that I love him and that I will find him and Fargo."

He heard a door slide open and suddenly something landed on his chest and licked his chin.

"Wurrah."

Jeff stroked Oola, who decided to curl up between his head and his shoulder and purr into his ear.

Jeff yawned and fell asleep.

8

Stand-off

Wearing altered space suits, Jeff and Albany carried their helmets over to Lizzie, who seemed the same except for an additional polish and what Jeff could have sworn was a pleased expression in her gleaming headlights.

Rembrandt waited beside the taxi, holding a remarkably placid Oola in his lower arms. Rembrandt's strangely humanoid face was sad. "Should I not go with you?"

"No," Albany said firmly. "If we rescue Fargo there won't be much room for all of us in Lizzie. Take care of Oola for us. She's usually quite good, and she obviously likes you."

Oola yawned and went to sleep, one paw draped possessively over Rembrandt's arm.

Lizzie's headlights swiveled to look at Rembrandt. "I am pleased, kind sir Other, that your marvelous technicians were able to install my new capacities inside my trunk and hood without disturbing my outward shape."

"Thank you, Lizzie."

"But sir Other, the existence of your people is supposed to be a secret, so what will I say when humans who don't know about you ask how my machinery was improved?"

Rembrandt's upper shoulders lifted. "I do not know. Does anyone have any suggestions?"

"Lizzie's legal owners are my stepmother's family," Albany said. "We can say that they always wanted a taxi equipped with spaceship machinery to provide additional air. That happens to be true. We'll just omit how it happened."

Rembrandt smiled at Albany but she did not smile back.

"You've kept us long enough, Rembrandt. Let's go, Jeff."

47

It was easy to understand Albany's anger at being put to sleep against her will, but Jeff felt he had to stick up for Rembrandt. "Albany, the delay has made me anxious, too, but Rembrandt was right to help us enter Federation space in a vehicle that's capable of keeping us alive for longer than a normal taxi could."

"I know, Jeff, and I appreciate the effort." She turned to Rembrandt. "I apologize for my irritability, but I'm worried. Will this ship actually be able to send Lizzie and us out into normal space?"

"Yes, Albany."

"Without revealing the existence of this ship of the Others, how will we explain our method of leaving hyperspace?"

"I have an idea," Jeff said. "When Garc used Norby to hyperjump the stolen taxis away from Earth, we were pulled along into hyperspace. If asked how we got out, we'll just say that Lizzie was hurled out of hyperspace in a manner we don't understand. That's true, too, because you and I and Lizzie can't understand how Yib's going to do it."

"Sir Other, I can hardly believe that, thanks to Yib, I will enter normal space near Computer Prime—at the near edge of the asteroid belt. Who would have believed that an old Manhattan taxi would ever see such strange territory?"

"Hardly strange," Albany said sarcastically. "That part of the asteroid belt has been heavily mined—and littered. Some of it looks like a garbage dump."

"Is that not dangerous for Computer Prime?" asked Rembrandt.

"Computer Prime's in a cleared area, to prevent collisions that might damage its metal hull, although I understand it's very thick and strong. Our space engineers have even managed to move some of the bigger asteroids that were predicted to hit Earth at any time in the future. We don't want to disappear like the dinosaurs."

"Is Computer Prime inhabited?" Rembrandt asked.

"No, although there are living quarters for human

inspectors. . . . Jeff! If Garc gets inside, he could hide out there indefinitely! We must leave at once and warn the Federation. If Garc is out to control the Federation, he'll control Computer Prime first. . . ."

"And with Norby's hyperdrive he could have beaten us there. He could already be bollixing everything up with that almost magical Connector ring of his," Jeff added.

"And he might use my husband, who's something of a computer expert. My darling is in danger and I want to go to him *now*."

"And so you will, Albany," Rembrandt said. "Yib is ready to send your taxi into normal space. One more thing. Lizzie's hycom equipment has been improved so that she can now reach Yib while either or both of them are in normal space or hyperspace."

"Then if Jeff and I become desperate, we'll call for help. Only then should you risk being seen taking your ship out of hyperspace, Rembrandt."

"I will monitor your progress through one of the channels of Lizzie's hycom. Do not turn it off."

Albany got inside Lizzie. "Okay, okay, Rembrandt. Hurry up, Jeff."

As Jeff entered the taxi and was closing the door, he heard Rembrandt say, "Remember that although you will have more air, the supply is still limited. We do not know how long it will last, for there was not time to calibrate the mechanism for human oxygen consumption as opposed to ours. . . ."

"Go, Lizzie!" Albany yelled.

Directly ahead, the metallic surface of Computer Prime showed a few pits from micrometeorite collisions, but what caught Jeff's attention was the ring-shaped design.

"My colleagues are trapped," Lizzie said mournfully.

As the taxi went closer, Jeff realized that the design was a circle of vehicles, mainly Manhattan taxis along with some unmanned and probably stolen space trucks and garbage scows, their noses pressed against Computer Prime like strange beetles frozen in the battle to push a gigantic ball of dung.

Computer Prime was slowly rotating, but Lizzie's tracking device kept her facing the horrible design. Her visual sensors were more efficient than human eyes, so she spotted the other horror before Jeff did.

"Look, kind humans, there are small industrial robots and packages of brain components in between—and touching—each vehicle! How awful! But I do not see Norby or Jonesy."

"What's that villain done with my husband?" Albany yelled.

A resonant tenor voice answered. "Hi, there, my sweet. It's gratifying to have a bride who worries about me."

"Fargo! Darling! Where are you?"

"Rotating behind you."

Jeff and Albany turned as one. Lined up at presumably a safe distance from Computer Prime was what looked like the entire fleet of Space Command, with little Jonesy in front.

"Darling!"

"Albany, my love, it is not a good idea to be that close to Computer Prime. Come to your ever-faithful husband, not that I've been your husband very long, but I did promise to be faithful. . . ."

"And of course you are. Lizzie, take us to my husband."

"Yes, Lieutenant." Lizzie moved backward toward Jonesy, as if she were reluctant to turn her rear end to the threat on Computer Prime.

Jeff could see Fargo at the viewport, beckoning eagerly.

"Get us near Jonesy's airlock, Lizzie," Albany said as she put on her suit's helmet. "You'd better put on your helmet, too, Jeff. We'll join Fargo in a real spaceship."

"And leave me alone?" Lizzie wailed.

"You hang around, Lizzie," Jeff said, trying to placate her as he fastened his helmet.

"Cadet Wells and Lieutenant Jones, I trust you are well?" The bass voice boomed out from Lizzie's speakers.

"Yes, Admiral Yobo," Albany said. "We were . . . sort of . . . dragged this far by Garc—I'm afraid I can't explain by what means. But how did you get here so fast from Earth?"

"Matter transporters. From Earth to Luna City, from there to Mars, and on to one of the artificial space settlements near the asteroid belt, where I'd told my fleet to assemble. Our shields are on full force, and at this distance, Garc apparently can't affect our computers."

"But how did you and Jonesy escape, Fargo?" asked Jeff.

Fargo laughed. He usually did, when there was danger. "It was easy, chum. After Garc's taxis landed here to join in that ring he's built, I decided I'd better take Jonesy's brain apart and handle the ship manually. I'm good at flying by the seat of my pants and it was the only way to get out of that unholy web that Garc has created. Once out, I called the Admiral. And my new father-in-law, but Leo said you and Albany had left."

"We're here now, darling," Albany said, helping Jeff with his balky helmet. "I suppose that Computer Prime is now part of whatever kind of web Garc has built."

"Yes, and the Federation is probably falling apart."

"Not so!" Yobo argued. "Merely inconvenienced. The Solarweb functions without a central library computer."

"Functions poorly," Fargo said.

"Harumph, somewhat. Many of my hycom calls to Space Command seem to be lost in transit somewhere."

Albany finally managed to close Jeff's helmet. "At last, we're ready. Open your top, Lizzie."

Albany pushed herself easily across the space between Lizzie and Jonesy, entering the ship's airlock.

"Hurry up, Jeff," Fargo said, "and when you get here, try reaching Norby on hycom. The whole thing is his fault. I can't believe Garc could have done this mischief without Norby's help."

"Norby wouldn't do anything to harm the Federation if he could help it!"

"Little brother, perhaps your Norby is no longer Norby."

"That being so," said Yobo, "we are going to destroy the vehicles around Computer Prime, one by one. Scanners show none contain organic beings, so we won't be killing a person. I hope we won't be destroying a robot like Norby, but if that's what it takes to free Computer Prime, then we'll have to do it."

"Let me try to talk to Norby first!"

"Very well, Cadet, but hurry."

Jeff suddenly made up his mind. "I want to stay in Lizzie to use her hycom, Admiral. It's been, uh, improved recently, by a painter friend of ours who, uh, stayed home."

"I understand, Cadet. Go ahead."

Jeff took stock. Albany and Fargo were safely together inside their spaceship. Yobo was also safe inside his ship, backed by the firepower of the fleet, which would soon be aimed at the ring of vehicles and robots on Computer Prime.

"Norby! Norby! Answer me!"

"Jeff sir, there is no response on hycom."

"Do you feel any pull from the Connector?"

"Slightly, but I have a technique for counteracting the pull. I put most of my cognitive circuits to work on correlating the number and varieties of fares I have had in my lifetime, and since that is a good many years, the process acts as a blockage to this strange influence Garc has over computer brains."

"Good, Lizzie. Remember how you did that, so you can teach Norby, if we ever find him."

"But there is no response. Perhaps he has deactivated."

"I have to find out. I must rescue Norby."

"Don't try it, little brother," Fargo scolded. "Go any closer, and Lizzie's technique for blocking Garc's influence may not work."

Yobo's bass voice boomed out again. "Cadet, I order you to join us back here where it's safe. Since you cannot make contact with Norby, we must assume the worst—he is probably deactivated, or certainly under Garc's control."

"Admiral, please . . ."

"Jeff, I'm ordering the fleet to start destroying the circle of vehicles and robots, one by one. We can do that without penetrating the hull of Computer Prime, but we may eventually have to destroy all of it if that's the only way to stop Garc. Hurry over here."

"Hurry, Jeff," Albany said.

"Yes, Jeff," Fargo added. "You'll be safer in Jonesy, while Lizzie can stay with the fleet. Hurry."

Jeff gritted his teeth because it seemed to him that all the significant elders in his life persisted in telling him to hurry to safety.

His thoughts whirled. I don't care how dangerous it is. Maybe Lizzie's completely immune. Maybe Norby can reach me. . . .

"Admiral! First let me try to reach Norby one other way. You know how." He didn't dare say "telepathically" because that particular talent was also supposed to be a secret, and other people in the fleet might be listening to his conversation with the admiral.

"You've tried it."

"Not with Lizzie's hycom turned off. I must feel alone while I try."

"I'll give you ten minutes, Cadet. Then you and Lizzie must join the safety of the fleet."

Jeff switched off Lizzie's Federation hycom and settled himself on her rear seat, closing his eyes.

—Norby. Where are you? Norby, please answer.

There were no words, but a picture formed in Jeff's mind, and instantly vanished.

"Did you get that, Jeff sir?" asked Lizzie. "I saw a refrigerator in my mind, and the door opened, and then the image disappeared. What does it mean?"

"I saw the same thing. Once when we were home, I asked the servorobot for something from the refrigerator. It wasn't functioning properly and left the refrigerator door open. Norby repaired the servorobot."

"If Norby is trying to tell you that he is not functioning properly, we already know that."

"Maybe he's trying to let me know that I should pay attention to the door into Computer Prime. It must be in the center of the ring of vehicles because the surface looks smoother there. Yobo must have the code for opening the airlock. Can you extract it from his ship's computer, Lizzie?"

"Alas, kind Cadet, I do not have Norby's talents. You could ask the Admiral for it."

"He'll refuse. It's not only top secret but he and my brother and sister-in-law will say it's too dangerous to go in."

Another voice spoke. "Perhaps I can help, Jeff."

"Rembrandt? How can you be listening?"

"You turned off only the Federation channels. The one we installed is still open to me, and with no one else listening, I feel free to talk."

"How can you help?"

"I must confess that in my explorations of this part of the galaxy, I was curious about Computer Prime after its construction, so I, ah, that is, Yib and I . . ."

"Broke the code?"

"Yes. When no one was around, I went in and downloaded Computer Prime's stored information. If Computer Prime is destroyed, we will give it to the Federation. Take me with you, Jeff. Don't go into Computer Prime alone."

"No way, Rembrandt. Just imagine what the fleet will think if your ship pops into this space. I'll go alone."

"The Admiral is prepared to fire upon Computer Prime."

"Let him demolish that circle of taxis. I'm going to find Norby. Give me the code."

9

Computer Prime

"Thanks for the code, Rembrandt."

"Good luck, Jeff."

"Let's go, Lizzie."

"Should we not inform Admiral Yobo, Jeff sir?"

"Not until it's too late for him to stop us."

"Maybe he should."

"Lizzie! Is that any way for a brave Manhattan taxi to talk? Considering the way you zip in and out of city air traffic patterns when the mood strikes you . . ."

"I know Manhattan. I do not know Computer Prime, and my cognitive circuits, the ones MacGillicuddy installed, are not vibrating with bravery. I confess that I am slightly terrified."

"As long as it's only slightly, we'll venture forth. I'm not going to let that villain Garc keep my Norby."

"Are we not going to rescue Computer Prime from Garc's clutches as well?"

"If we can. You've got the code, Lizzie, use it!"

As if she thought fast action would wipe out fear, Lizzie zoomed toward the center of the ring design.

When she was so close that Jeff could see the license plates on the taxis and garbage scows, the smooth center divided in half and each half opened outward like a blossoming flower.

"Cadet! What do you think you're doing! Garc must have stolen the codes for opening the door, so he's really inside and it's dangerous. Do not go in!"

Lizzie's tinny whisper was so faint that Jeff hardly heard her say, "I am required by law to notify authorities of the

55

destination of each fare, so I turned on the Federation hycom."

"I'm not a fare, blast it!"

"What was that, Cadet? Are you swearing at your Admiral?"

"No, sir. Now that the door is open, I must go inside to rescue Norby. I'll try to come out right away."

"Wait for me, little brother." Jonesy moved away from the fleet armada and came toward Lizzie.

"Oh, no—Fargo, let me go alone. You and Albany should not risk yourselves."

"I'm responsible for you, Jeff. I assume you're determined to rescue Norby before the Admiral's fireworks begin, but Albany and I are going to help. Once inside Computer Prime, Lizzie's computer brain may be captured by Garc's connector, but Jonesy's on manual."

"Okay, Fargo. The door's open and we're going in, so hurry up." It was a distinct pleasure to tell someone else to hurry.

Lizzie flew easily through the enormous opening into Computer Prime's airlock, a wide tube that stretched through the thick walls. The metal tube wall was dotted with sensors, machinery, and various grappling devices in case an inspection ship had to stay there to repair the tube itself.

"Jeff sir! The airlock door is closing!"

"Fargo! Hurry!"

"I see it. Jonesy's at top speed so we'll—" Fargo's sentence was cut off as the outer door of the airlock shut.

"Fargo, I'll try to—"

"No use, Jeff sir. The hycom does not function."

"I didn't hear a crash so Fargo must have turned Jonesy aside in time. We must let them in. Open the airlock door, Lizzie."

"I am not able to comply. The access code no longer opens the outer door. Is not this airlock supposed to be filling with air now that we are inside?"

"Yes. It isn't?"

"No, sir."

"Go to the inner door and try opening that."

As Lizzie flew through the tube, Jeff tried to assure himself that there would be plenty of air inside Computer Prime itself and anyway, the taxi now had a good air supply.

But for how much time? Suddenly Jeff felt as if he were choking. The suit's air supply had malfunctioned! He tore off the helmet as quickly as he could and took deep breaths of the air inside the taxi.

"Lizzie, does the hycom to Yib work?"

"No, sir. I have been trying to reach Yib, but without success. I do not know if Garc is blocking our transmissions or if the nature of the airlock is such that we cannot transmit beyond it. Here is the door of the inner lock."

There was a short pause. "I am sorry, sir, but the code will not open it."

Jeff tried not to panic, but he couldn't help thinking that the airlock tube was beginning to seem like a huge coffin.

"Jeff sir . . ."

"Be quiet for a moment, Lizzie. I'm going to try reaching Norby telepathically."

In the silence of the taxi and the lifeless airlock outside, Jeff felt as if his own heartbeat and breathing sounded loud and strange. He tried to concentrate.

—Norby. Lizzie and I are trapped in Computer Prime's airlock. Please let us inside. I want to rescue you.

At first nothing happened, then a brief image flickered in Jeff's mind and disappeared.

"I saw an image of Rembrandt," he told Lizzie. "Norby must be telling me to get help from him, only we can't."

"I do not know what that means, sir, but perhaps the Others are of some help anyway."

"They can't help! We're out of communication. . . ."

"Excuse me for interrupting, kind human sir, but the circuits you humans use for emotive capabilities are probably too overloaded at the moment for you to think clearly."

"Lizzie! This is no time to lecture a passenger, even if I'm a nonpaying fare!"

"Indeed, Jeff sir. I am merely trying to tell you that Yib gave me more than the airlock access code, which Garc seems to have changed to keep us out. I have the access code to Computer Prime itself."

"Why haven't you used it?"

"Computer Prime is under the control of Garc. I do not know if gaining access to Computer Prime's cognitive circuits will be dangerous for you, Jeff sir."

Jeff sat back in Lizzie's pliable, comforting rear seat, and gave the problem some thought.

"Lizzie, maybe Norby knew that Rembrandt had entered Computer Prime in the past, with access codes to the doors. . . . Oh, I'm so stupid! Rembrandt and Yib would have had to crack the access codes to Computer Prime itself, in order to download from its memory banks, and Norby guessed that. He wants us to tie in to Computer Prime."

"Garc may stop you."

"I'm sure he'll try. I can't believe Garc is benevolent, yet when he and his Connector ring stole those vehicles outside, nobody was hurt. Fargo wasn't killed when he put Jonesy on manual and escaped."

"Yes, yes, Jeff sir!" Lizzie said excitedly. "Garc is human, but we taxis, and in fact all vehicles, have robot brains that must obey the laws of robotics. Perhaps Garc has trouble taking enough control to override the laws of robotics embedded in computer brains."

"The question is, would that apply to Computer Prime? Use the other access code and let me speak to Computer Prime."

"Working. Speak now, Jeff sir."

"Computer Prime, I am a human trapped inside your airlock. Open the inner door so I can get inside where there is air. If you do not open the inner door, I will die and it will be your fault, Computer Prime. Obey the laws of robotics!"

The door opened and Lizzie sped into a large lighted space surrounded by patterned walls. Two viewscreens dominated the room. One looked toward the lights of stars, asteroids, and the outer planets in the blackness of space. The view was so clear that Jeff could see many of Jupiter's larger moons as points of light around the solar system's largest planet. The other viewscreen looked sunward, showing the Federation fleet lined up nearby, with Mars a blob of light far behind them.

Below a large, blank computer screen was an old-fashioned desk with a chair in front of it. Six folding chairs were stacked in a corner. There were also two doors, one closed at the far end, and another, directly opposite Jeff, open to show living quarters beyond.

"My sensors show that there is plenty of air here for you, Jeff sir."

"That's good." Jeff opened Lizzie's door and stepped out, marveling at the perfection of the artificial gravity that was needed only for human visitors. Or perhaps Garc had turned it on for his own convenience.

At that moment he had to make a dash for the living quarters and, after a struggle with his space suit, got there in time to use the excretory facilities. Lizzie could not squeeze into the corridor to follow him, for which he was thankful.

When he went back to the main room, she was waiting anxiously by the door. "Are you all right, kind Jeff sir?"

"I guess I'm more upset than I thought."

"You look pale."

"I'm sort of dizzy."

"Perhaps you are hungry. Rembrandt packed some food for you and the lieutenant, if you look under my front seat."

"Thanks, but I've never been sure that the food of the Others gives humans enough energy. I'll try the food replicator here." Along with a drink of very flat-tasting water, Jeff ate a dose of vitamins disguised in a chocolate chip health cookie. To his surprise, the cookie was delicious.

Munching it and feeling stronger, he joined Lizzie in the main room, where he tried the other door.

It was locked. "What's in here, Lizzie?"

"Scanning shows that it opens into the machinery and storage banks of the computer."

"Is Norby inside?"

"I cannot scan deeply. He is not nearby."

"Do you have access codes to this door?"

"No, sir."

"I suppose Rembrandt didn't need to get into Computer Prime's innards since all he wanted was the data. Well, use the access code to Computer Prime so it will answer me."

"I did so when we entered. Like most computers, Computer Prime is voice activated once the access code is given, so you may speak to it now, Jeff sir."

Jeff swallowed the last of his cookie and sat at the desk. "Computer Prime, I am Cadet Jefferson Wells, a member of the Solar Federation, with the proper access code. Reply to my questions. Where is the robot Norby?"

There was no answer.

"Where is Garc?"

No answer.

"Lizzie, can you tell if the channel is open? Did the access code work?"

"Yes to both questions. Computer Prime is required to answer you but it does not, so I surmise that Garc prevents communication. There is much danger to computer brains here, and I fear . . ." Her doors began to open and shut.

"Lizzie! What's happening to you?"

"I am endeavoring to block . . . Jeff sir . . . please help me. I cannot . . . I cannot . . ."

To Jeff's horror, Lizzie's internal and external lights went out and her headlight covers snapped shut. It was as if she had suddenly died.

"Lizzie! Answer me!" When she did not, Jeff tried to open her doors to get inside the taxi, but they were locked fast.

"Norby!" Jeff cried in despair. "Computer Prime! Help! Somebody help!"

"No one will help you." It was the voice of Garc, booming out from a hidden speaker. "You should not have entered Computer Prime. You will have to live here forever."

"Garc, if either of us stays inside Computer Prime much longer, Admiral Yobo will assume we are dead and if my brother can't get inside . . ."

"Look at the viewscreen. Your brother is in a space suit, trying to open the outer lock."

"Fargo! Help, Fargo!"

"He cannot hear you. See—he is not succeeding, and is now going back to his ship to rejoin the fleet. They are helpless before my power."

"The admiral is not helpless, Garc. He will probably try to destroy the vehicles in your ring."

As Jeff spoke, a bright light shot out of Admiral Yobo's ship and Computer Prime vibrated.

"Your admiral's efforts to fire upon me are ridiculous because I was going to leave anyway. Computer Prime and I don't like this part of the galaxy. I am sending a message to your admiral. You can listen, too."

"Federation fleet, attend! This is Garc the Great. You will have to build another Computer Prime, because I am removing this one and its new ring of power. Good-bye."

Both viewscreens shimmered for a moment. Then there was only the gray of hyperspace.

10

Going Backward

In the viewscreen, Jeff saw hyperspace for only a second before it vanished, replaced by a view of something big and . . .

"Garc! Computer Prime is going to crash into the Moon!"

"I see it, I see it!"

The view stabilized as Computer Prime, like a huge spaceship, went into an orbit that swung around the Moon's poles.

"Garc, why have we traveled from the asteroid belt to Earth's Moon? Did you do it on purpose?"

"Uh . . . merely a temporary stop. I'm on my way to the Oort Cloud at the edge of our solar system. I've always wanted to explore all those comets."

"Idiot! You've gone in the opposite direction."

"Look, boy, you can stop asking questions because I am Garc the Magnifi—I mean, Garc the Great, and I'm handling this trip just fine. I'd shut down communications between us, but right now that seems to be impossible."

There was a distinct edge in Garc's voice. Merely irritability, or fear as well? Jeff hoped that Norby was somehow preventing Garc from disabling the intercom.

Although both screens showed the Moon, one was a closer view of an area that Jeff recognized as the great South Pole–Aitken Basin. Aitken (as it was usually called at the Academy) was fifteen hundred kilometers in diameter, and was overlooked by a sunlit high mountain very useful to the Federation.

During his many travels, Jeff had seen all parts of the Moon, but this time Aitken looked very different. There were no immense solar power stations—the big man-made structures built to take advantage of the permanent sunlight on the mountain and the permanent shadow in parts of Aitken.

Jeff felt as if cold fingers gripped his neck. Those power stations were built in the middle of the twenty-first century, long before he was born.

"Garc! Listen to me! We've gone back in time."

"Time travel is impossible."

"There's no evidence of human settlement on the Moon. Ask Computer Prime for confirmation that we've traveled in time."

Jeff hoped that Computer Prime would not explain to Garc that it could time travel only because Norby was now part of it.

There was a long pause. Presumably Garc could communicate with Computer Prime without Jeff's hearing it.

Garc cleared his throat. "According to transmissions coming from Earth, we are now in the early twenty-first century, which of course I've planned all along."

"You're lying."

"Well, I've always wished I could go back to the time before Computer Prime was built. As I recall from my history reading, Computer Prime was first placed on the Moon and only later built into its present shape and moved to the asteroid belt."

Jeff was exasperated. "We should not be in this era. It's dangerous."

"Nonsense. I am pleased. By bringing Computer Prime here, I will speed up the development of the space age. With my Connector I will link Computer Prime to Earth's Solarweb."

"You don't know your history. At this time, there is no Solarweb, only something called the World Wide Web. Humanity still lives only on Earth, Garc!"

"Fine. I've ordered Computer Prime to link up. . . . Why not?"

Another voice answered him—deep, resonant, yet with a

metallic tinge to it. Computer Prime had begun to speak not only to Garc but in the room where Jeff was trapped. Had Norby made that possible? Jeff could only hope.

"Master Garc, if the Connector links up Earth's computers during this time period they will be destroyed because they are not strong enough to withstand the force of the connection."

"Do it anyway," Garc said querulously. "I'll show Earth how to start over, with me in charge."

"You'll change history!" Jeff yelled.

Garc sniffed. "History should be changed."

"Master Garc, information now available to me shows that changing history in this manner will certainly delay for many years the development of a genuinely global web of computer cyberspace, usable by all humanity."

"Not if I create a new web!" Garc shouted.

"Furthermore, a much worse scenario could occur, Master Garc. In this time period, the destruction of computer services over the entire planet Earth will probably cause the collapse of Terran civilization. Colonization of the solar system may never occur, or will be delayed for centuries."

"Why? You'll be here to fix everything, Computer Prime."

"I must correct you, Master Garc. I will be unable to function in this time period because no computer will exist to provide access to me."

"Doesn't matter. Earth will accept me as its hero, and I'll be famous forever. You just have to do everything I want. We'll take the Connector to Earth and show them how to make better computers in this backward century."

Jeff could stand it no longer. "Garc, don't you know anything about the laws of robotics, which . . ."

This time he was interrupted by Computer Prime, giving Jeff more hope that Norby was behind the conversation. The only artificial intelligence likely to interrupt a human was Norby.

"Master Garc, you may try to make me obey your Connector, yet I cannot obey both it and the laws of robotics when the Connector violates the laws and endangers the lives of human beings. I repeat, if you use the Connector in this time period, you will probably die."

"Why?"

"By destroying the computer networks now on Earth you will prevent the original version of myself from being built at the correct time. If that happens, I may disappear and you humans will die in space here. I cannot allow that."

Jeff held his breath. Garc could not possibly know that what Computer Prime—or Norby—had just said might not be true. Norby could survive in the past even if the time line had been changed. But Norby, through Computer Prime, had not really lied, for he had no way of knowing whether or not Computer Prime could survive.

Jeff knew from his own experience that when you changed the past, you might not be able to exist in your own time. The trick was to undo the mistake, and Jeff did not trust Garc to be willing or able to admit, much less undo, his mistakes.

"Obey me, Computer Prime," Garc yelled.

"The laws of robotics . . ."

"Forget them!"

Jeff shouted, "Garc, you should thank your lucky stars for those laws. Computer Prime's trying to stop you from making a terrible mistake that could kill us."

Garc's voice became a frightened screech. "You don't understand! Holding the Connector, I feel that it wants to go back . . . back, back, to stop something terrible."

"Stop what?"

"I don't know. Death. Some sort of death."

"Garc, ask it—"

"Stupid boy, I can't communicate with the Connector."

"You've been pretending to."

"I know but"—Garc was whining now—"the Connector is

so hard to control! When I found we really had time traveled, I thought if I put the Connector to work here in this time period, it would be distracted and forget about going further back."

There was a tremendous lurch, and hyperspace again appeared in the viewscreens. Jeff hammered on the locked door to the rest of Computer Prime. "Let me in, Garc! I'll try to help you control the Connector, or help Computer Prime resist it."

The door opened so fast that Jeff almost fell into what seemed like an endless hallway, although he knew it was less than a couple of kilometers. As he righted himself and prepared to walk the length, he heard Lizzie behind him.

"Jeff sir, I am awake again, for I have been released from the temporary hold the Connector had because I am so close to it and as part of Computer Prime it is stronger now. I was released because the Connector is concentrating on something else. I advise you to get inside, for the corridor you are in is big enough for me and you will not have to walk."

Gratefully, he patted Lizzie's hood and got inside. She flew through the corridor, past rows of doors.

"Not so fast, Lizzie. We have to find Garc and he may be behind one of these doors."

"Jeff sir, I am using my sensors, fully operational now that we are out of the entry space. I think that Sir Rembrandt improved my sensors for I can tell that there is machinery behind all these doors. The only human being is in a room at the other end of this corridor."

"Then go ahead."

Soon some of the side doors were transparent, showing Jeff Computer Prime's innards, bigger and more complicated than any artificial brain and memory center he'd ever seen.

Lizzie pulled up before the door at the end of the corridor. It opened onto what was obviously the command center for Computer Prime. Lizzie rolled in and Jeff got out.

The circular room was covered with instrument panels, computer screens, and holoviewscreens. Stuck on the control panel was the Connector ring, gripped tightly by a small, thin man with a wispy gray beard and unhappy gray eyes.

"I'm Jeff Wells, Garc. You're in a lot of trouble and I think you should let go of the Connector."

"I can't. It won't let me. After I found it on a distant asteroid I was going to sell it, but it had other plans."

"Where is Norby, my robot?"

"Up there. I didn't do it. The Connector did."

Norby was suspended from the high ceiling by his antenna. His arms, legs, and head were closed up in his barrel body.

"Jeff Wells, I didn't intend . . . that is, I didn't mean to do anything really bad. I just wanted to help Computer Prime and I thought that's what the Connector would do."

"Help it? By stealing robots, including mine?"

"I wanted the robots to make Computer Prime even bigger, and then it turned out that the Connector needed them . . . to make connections. I mean—it doesn't tell me, but I sort of know what it wants."

"And when did you decide it wanted my robot, Garc?"

"You see, I was in my old gar—that is, my ship, near Space Command, having a little fun with graffiti. . . ."

"We saw that."

"Yeah. Anyway, I suddenly felt that the Connector needed the robot belonging to Cadet Wells. I was going to . . . well, I couldn't, because you left—I don't know how. Then the Connector made me go to Earth to get Norby, but my ship would have taken too long and besides, it broke down so I had to spend a lot of money using the Mars-to-Earth transporter."

"Then you stole the taxis and Norby."

"Yes, and found I could travel through hyperspace even quicker than the transporters. I don't know why."

Jeff did not enlighten him about Norby's talents. He reentered Lizzie.

"What are you going to do?" asked Garc.

"Get help. Lizzie, up to Norby, please."

"Yes, sir. I think Norby is now blocking the Connector's power over me."

"I hope so, Lizzie. That's it—as close as possible."

Opening Lizzie's roof door, Jeff reached up to touch Norby.

—This is Jeff. I'm here.

—It's about time you showed up.

11

Time Changed

—Norby! You're you!

—Who else could I be?

—I thought you were part of Computer Prime now.

—I am. That is, Computer Prime is partly me.

—Then how can we talk like this?

—I don't know. When you're touching me, Jeff, I seem to be able to talk to you as myself. Only I'm also part of Computer Prime at the same time. It's a little hard to explain since it's all due to that Connector.

—How does the Connector work?

—I hate to admit it, but I don't understand the Connector at all. It's a very strange device. And very powerful. It has forced me to use my time-travel talent to . . . oops, sorry, but here we go again!

Computer Prime seemed to shudder, and hyperspace vanished from the viewscreens. The Moon reappeared, but now it was much farther away, and Earth was closer. Jeff barely had a chance to notice that Earth's continents were not like those of his own time, when there was a tremendous crash.

Below Jeff and Lizzie, Garc let go of the Connector and fell off his chair, moaning.

Above Jeff, Norby's antenna retracted and he fell.

"I'm keeping steady," Lizzie said. "Catch Norby!"

"Did it," Jeff said, collapsing onto Lizzie's backseat with Norby in his arms. "Close your roof door, Lizzie."

"Yes, sir. Shall we leave?"

"We'd better," said Norby. "The Connector doesn't need me anymore and I can take you both to safety."

Jeff was conscious of an outside shift to gray and then Lizzie was hanging in space just above Earth's atmosphere, all alone, for there was no Computer Prime nearby.

"We're back in our own century," Norby announced as his half a head emerged from his barrel. "Thanks to my talent."

Jeff looked down at the continents. "Earth's continents are correct. Unfortunately we didn't bring Computer Prime and Garc with us. We should not have left them behind."

"Had to, Jeff. Something was adding to Computer Prime's mass, and I could not have brought it with me easily, if at all. I have marvelous hyperdrive power, but, well . . ."

"It's limited," Jeff said, thinking rapidly. Would it endanger Norby to return to the same era where the Connector was?

"I think it will endanger me, Jeff. Sorry, but I'm sitting on your lap and can read your mind a little when we're touching, especially if your thoughts are strong. I'm sorry about Computer Prime. The Federation will have to build another one."

"Norby, Garc is trapped in Computer Prime, millions of years ago. It was the Cretaceous period, wasn't it?"

"That's right. Perhaps the dinosaurs will eat Garc."

Lizzie squawked, "For shame, Norby! You disobey the law!"

"Lizzie's right," Jeff said. "What's happened to *your* laws of robotics, Norby?"

"They have been severely overstrained. Lizzie, I think you should take Jeff and me straight to our Manhattan apartment so we can recuperate while notifying Fargo and the admiral, who will help us decide what to do about Garc the Great."

"Shall I do so, Jeff sir?"

"Okay, Lizzie. I could do with a quiet rest before we go on a rescue mission, if it's possible."

"And hurry up, Lizzie," Norby ordered.

She went down through the atmosphere so fast that the temperature inside the taxi rose. Jeff began to sweat and the windows fogged up. By the time Lizzie had cleared the windows, they were above a city.

"This should be Manhattan Island," Lizzie said. "The shape seems the same, but the city does not look right."

"Then this can't be the correct time period," Jeff said. "You've made a mistake in time traveling, Norby."

"I have not. I'm sure I've brought us to our own century. Geologically this is definitely Manhattan Island. Unfortunately, the city is not like the one we know."

"That's putting it mildly," Jeff said as Lizzie flew low over the city. Except for the various valleys, hills, and rock outcroppings natural to Manhattan, the land was covered by one-story oval buildings separated by wide cement paths.

"It's old," Norby said.

Everywhere, weeds and scrubby bushes had taken root in cracks of the paths. Many of the buildings were festooned with vines, some had collapsed into rubble, and many seemed on the verge of falling down.

"There have never been skyscrapers here," Jeff muttered. "This strange city has been deserted for a long time."

"Oh, dear," Lizzie wailed. "I want my Manhattan! Could we have gone by mistake into the far future?"

"I doubt it, Lizzie. Something would have remained of the old human-built Manhattan. And we can't be in the past because there was never a city of Manhattan that looked like this. What have you done, Norby?"

"It's not my fault!"

"Maybe, maybe not. Lizzie, go up one of those paths and find a building that doesn't seem ready to collapse. Gosh, I can see spiderwebs over the ruins."

"Have you noticed that those red spiders are as big as dinner plates?" Norby asked.

"Yes, and they're catching fairly large flying insects," Jeff said. "The spiders seem to be the biggest organisms around. I don't see any birds or mammals, not even a mouse."

"That is correct," Lizzie said. "My scanners show that the only land creatures are insects. As I was descending to Earth I scanned the ocean, and there were no fish. Only bacteria and invertebrates. What has happened to this planet?"

"I don't know," Jeff said. "Insects could not have built the city, so we have to find out who did. Lizzie, stop at that big building. It seems intact."

When Lizzie came to a halt and lowered herself to the path, Jeff reached to open the taxi's door. It was locked.

"Open your door, Lizzie."

"I cannot, Jeff sir. The outside air may be dangerous to you. Norby, tie in to my computer system and check on the data from my scanners."

"She's right, Jeff," Norby said after plugging in. "Better stay inside."

"But I want to get out. There aren't any big predators here, and the air looks clean enough to me. I feel like walking, and I want to explore that big building. The spiderwebs over the door have been broken, so something's gone in."

"No, Jeff sir, you must stay here for safety."

"But I don't think there are any animals here as big as a human. I'll keep out of the way of the spiders in case they are poisonous." Jeff tried again to open the door.

Norby tugged at Jeff's arm. "You must stay in Lizzie's sealed chassis."

"Then you go outside, Norby, and . . ."

"No, Jeff. I cannot go out to investigate because I would have to open the door, which would let in outside air. Lizzie's scanners show that the air has dust that contains infectious spores. It's something like a peculiar virus, only worse."

"Infectious to me?"

"I don't know, but we can't take a chance. Lizzie, that doorway's big enough for you, so you can take Jeff and me inside the building Jeff wants to see."

Barging through, Lizzie tore a bigger hole in the doorway's

72

spiderweb. She turned on her lights and floated on antigrav through a short corridor into a large room full of equipment.

"There are no marks on the floor," Jeff said. "Somebody's cleaned out the dust."

Lizzie said, "If those squiggles on the equipment are words, I do not recognize the language, but I have never seen the written language of the Others. Is that it?"

"No," Jeff said. "I can't read it."

Norby's eyelids flickered. "But I can, a little. I think I must have acquired the knowledge from the Connector. This is a computerized library—something like Computer Prime, only smaller. I think I could access the data if I try, but I don't dare open the door and let air in to you, Jeff."

"I will try to access the data," Lizzie said, "and you can get it from me."

Norby told Lizzie where to insert a wire, and after several tries, she said, "I think I'm tied in to this odd computer."

Norby plugged into Lizzie's computer again, shutting both his back and front set of eyes. It took a long time.

Jeff couldn't stand it. "Are you all right, Norby?"

Norby withdrew his antenna and opened his eyes. "My emotive circuits are not doing well. . . ."

"What do you mean? Have you been damaged?"

"My emotive circuits are intact, but agitated. The prevailing emotion is one of sadness."

"Why? What have you learned?"

"Not much, but enough. Lizzie, please poke that panel marked in blue."

When Lizzie's wire touched the blue panel, it slid back to open a wide shelf in the wall.

Lizzie rolled backward so quickly that Jeff and Norby were thrown to her floor. "I am sorry, kind sirs, but I was surprised by what I saw."

"Don't worry, Lizzie," Jeff said. "It's only a skeleton."

Curled up on the shelf was a skeleton about the size of Jeff, but the more that Jeff looked at it, the more he knew it was not a human being. Although it had two arms and two legs, the pelvis was oddly shaped and the neck too long. . . .

"Norby! It's got a bony snout on the skull, and isn't that a medium-sized tail at the end of the backbone?"

"Yes, and the hands have only two fingers and a thumb. Did you notice the message on the wall above the skeleton?"

This time the squiggly writing looked as if it had been done by hand, and very shakily.

"Can you read that, Norby?" Jeff asked.

"With difficulty. The skeleton is apparently a female who left a message saying that she decided to die here in the library she loved rather than join the rest of her species in the death ships to be sunk at sea. Lizzie's scanners show that this happened about five thousand years ago."

"But who . . ."

"She was the last librarian of her civilization. They called themselves—in that alien language—'The People.' According to her anatomy, her ancestors were probably late Cretaceous maniraptors, much changed."

Jeff swallowed hard. "An intelligent, civilized dinosaur!"

Lizzie swayed a little. "Kind sirs, please explain. I know I am only a Manhattan taxi, not a highly intelligent being, but I have seen holov documentaries that said dinosaurs were never very intelligent. I thought they became extinct at the end of the Cretaceous period, sixty-five million years ago."

"That should have happened, Lizzie," said Jeff. "Norby, was there any information in the dinosaurs' computer on how they avoided extinction?"

"I managed to retrieve only a sketch of their history. It did not mention any natural catastrophe in the distant past. But I did gather that sixty-five million years ago, those particular dinosaurs became both intelligent and civilized *all at once,* after they received something called the 'Gift of the Exile.' "

"What could that mean? Was there any indication that it's part of their mythology?"

"I don't know, Jeff. It's even stranger that although the dinosaurs had computers and other hallmarks of advanced civilization, they did not develop space travel, never left Earth, and of course never colonized the solar system."

"Gosh, after human civilization began, we went into space only a few thousand years later. The intelligent dinosaurs had many millions of years to develop space flight."

"They were busy, Jeff. Always making war on each other. The librarian's final words were something like 'We should have worked for peace, but instead we caused the Great Dying.'"

Lizzie backed a little farther from the skeleton. "I do not like this place or this time. Why is it not possible to go to our correct time, and my own sort of Manhattan Island, full of magnificent buildings, beautiful parks, and eager fares?"

"Because they don't exist, Lizzie," Jeff said wearily. "This is a different time line. Something has changed history."

Lizzie's horn blared. "Four beings are entering the building. Jeff sir, I am sorry to inform you that I do not carry weapons, so unfortunately you are unarmed. Please remain inside and do not panic."

"It's all right, Lizzie," Norby said. "If they are dangerous, I'll just take you and Jeff into hyperspace."

Four humanoids walked in, and Jeff smiled, for he recognized the tallest one of them. "Rembrandt!"

Hearing the sound, the tall Other took out what could only be a gun.

"Norby," Jeff whispered. "He doesn't seem friendly."

The Other proceeded to aim the gun at Lizzie.

12

Another Rembrandt

The oldest Other, a shorter person with a wrinkled face, touched the one who looked like Rembrandt and spoke to him in his own language, which Jeff, Norby, and Lizzie could understand.

"That mechanism may be the small spaceship our sensors detected entering the planet's atmosphere. There seems to be an organic being inside. Perhaps we should try communicating."

"I am not a spaceship!" shouted Lizzie in Terran Basic. "I am a *taxi*! And have you forgotten me, Rembrandt?"

"This mechanism speaks and may be dangerous. I think it should be disabled."

Trying hard not to panic, Jeff whispered, "He can't understand you, Lizzie. We must use his language."

In the language of the Others, Jeff said, "Please do not shoot. We mean you no harm. I am an organic being, a human named Jeff Wells. Next to me is my robot, Norby. We are sitting in an intelligent vehicle named Lizzie. The tallest of you Others is named . . ." Jeff switched to Terran Basic. "Norby, I can't pronounce Rembrandt's real name."

Norby hopped into the front seat so the Others could see him better. "You are . . ." When Norby pronounced Rembrandt's real name, the Other lowered the gun and spoke.

"Where do you come from? How do you know my name? Are you archaeologists like us?"

"I call you Rembrandt, after a famous human artist, because you are a painter and sculptor, are you not?" Jeff asked.

"You know much about me. I am the artist on this archaeological expedition. We Others do not interfere with ongoing civilizations, but we study planets where there was once intelligent life." His three eyes seemed to grow larger and shinier, as if filled with unshed tears. "The intelligent life on this planet died long ago."

"That happened because this is the wrong time line," Jeff said. "Lizzie and Norby and I come from the right time line, in which we know you. In traveling through time, we have somehow changed history."

"Time travel is impossible."

"I'm afraid it is very possible. I'll try to explain what has happened." Jeff told the Others everything that had happened since he'd left the Academy for Fargo's wedding.

". . . so by taking Computer Prime to the Cretaceous, Garc has changed Earth's history. I've lost my brother, my new sister-in-law, and my admiral. . . ." Jeff's voice cracked. "In fact, I'm the only one left of my entire species. I can't go home because it doesn't exist."

A younger Other said, "Your story is so far-fetched that it is difficult to believe it."

"Our story is true," Norby said, "and I'll prove it." He launched into a detailed description of the Other's ship, including the computer Yib. "You see, we really have been in your ship, on another time line."

"Then it seems we must believe you," said Rembrandt. "I will tell you what we have learned of the history of the creatures you call dinosaurs. Their ancestors were given advanced technology by a being called the Exile, who arrived from the sky."

Norby touched Jeff.

—In a round spaceship, I'll bet.

"The dinosaurs were not creative, and remained dependent on a technology they had not developed themselves. A few learned how to repair the technology, but they never invented the means to space flight. They also overpopulated, controlling their numbers only through war. Near the end, the dinosaurs discovered a way of killing each other through disease."

"How horrible!" Jeff said.

"Each side immunized itself against the disease they sent, but the disease mutated, attacking everyone. When the population was down to a dying few, they made peace and drowned themselves in the ocean. All but the librarian."

"Could my human passenger catch this disease?" asked Lizzie.

"Are you a vertebrate, Jeff Wells?"

"Yes, I have a bony skeleton just as the dinosaurs did."

"Is your vehicle admitting outside air?"

"No, because we've detected unusual spores in the air."

"Keep your vehicle closed. The spores are infectious, attacking any vertebrate. Leave this infected world. Most of our species now live in ships, but a few remain on our planet, where you will be welcomed. I will give you its coordinates."

"I know them," Norby said.

"Norby," said Lizzie, "we must follow Rembrandt's advice and take Jeff at once to a place where he can live safely."

The oldest looking of the four Others suddenly sat down, leaning against the nearby wall as if exhausted.

"First I must tell you the rest of our findings," Rembrandt said. "We discovered that this building is not only a library but a shrine. Taxi Lizzie, I advise you to elevate."

As Lizzie hovered, he touched a wall switch and a section of floor slid back to make a narrow entry into what seemed to be a huge, dark cavern that brightened to show that the walls were white and studded with gems.

"Your vehicle will not fit through that opening, but we Others have explored inside. Tilt yourself, Lizzie, so your passengers can see."

From Lizzie's tilted window, Jeff now saw that in the center of the pit was the same round, spiky alien ship that had fired upon *The Hopeful*.

"The city was built around this ship, called *The Abode of the Exile*. We doubt that the dinosaurs would have—or could have—broken the lock code to enter the shrine, even after the Exile disappeared into it forever."

"Did you break the code?" asked Norby.

As if terribly tired, Rembrandt also sat down. "Yes. The ship contains the desiccated body of the Exile, holding a large golden ring-shaped device. I touched it, but it warned me away."

Norby jiggled excitedly up and down. "It all makes sense now. The Connector forced Garc to make Computer Prime more powerful. I was forced to take Computer Prime back sixty-five million years so it would collide with and change the course of the asteroid that was supposed to hit Earth. Any record of that asteroid in the Exile's computer?"

Rembrandt said, "The Exile noted that an asteroid was heading for Earth but she was afraid to try diverting it. She set her ship on course for the next solar system, expecting to die in space, but suddenly the asteroid hit something and veered away. Then the asteroid and the object with which it collided both headed for this planet's sun."

Jeff was horrified. What a terrible way for Garc to die.

"Since the planet was now safe, the Exile stayed here," Rembrandt continued. "She bioengineered the dinosaurs, giving them her own civilization, unfortunately a culture of war."

—Jeff, are you all right? You look pale.

—Maybe it's my imagination, Norby, but I think I'm having trouble getting enough air.

—We must leave.

—Norby, we killed Garc. He died in Computer Prime, unable to control it without you.

"I do not like all these comings and goings," Lizzie said. "Where did the Exile come from, sir Other?"

"Are you aware that there are many different universes that are ordinarily closed to one another?"

"Yes," Jeff said. "I've been to one of the other universes, but the Exile must have come from a different one. Do the Exile's records show how and why she came to this universe?"

"Her species never left their own solar system because they never invented hyperdrive. As they fought each other for living space, one tribe invented a way of traveling to another universe. The secret was stolen by another tribe so two ships entered this universe. They fought each other, and one ship was destroyed. Everyone in the surviving ship also died, except one female."

"Stupid to kill each other," Jeff said, feeling woozy.

"Indeed," Rembrandt said wryly. "Intelligence is not always correlated with wisdom."

"Why didn't the surviving ship go back home?" Norby asked.

"It proved to be impossible."

Lizzie seemed to quiver. "I am only a taxi, and I am sorry for the dinos and the Exile but I want my Manhattan back, full of human beings like Jeff here, who, by the way, is getting short of breath. And sir Other, are you well? Should you not return to your ship?"

"I didn't detect your ship in orbit," Norby said.

"Our ship has left. We are exiled here."

Jeff gasped. "Yib—I mean your ship's computer—wouldn't do such a thing."

"We told the ship to leave, to save the remaining crew and the artworks aboard our ship. We four were the landing party that came to inspect this planet's ruins. We found spores but we did not think they could infect aliens to this world. We were wrong. The spores can mutate to invade any vertebrate, where they live in—we call it klutal, the lining of joints and the entire skeleton in early vertebrates."

"Cartilage," Jeff said. "A tissue containing collagen."

Rembrandt wiped his forehead with one of his upper hands. "Our cartilage is not exactly like yours, but became infected. Inside the body, the spores produce a poison that eventually kills the organism. We have been infected for only one seasonal cycle, but we are weak and soon to die."

"Can't you find a cure?"

"We have not been successful. The dinosaurs did their terrible work well."

"Norby!" Jeff yelled, "We must find Garc and the Connector in the Cretaceous and restore the real time line. Then, Rembrandt, you'll be the Other that we know, who isn't infected and who isn't going to die."

"I wish you success," said the Other. "But be careful."

13

Vacation?

Jeff felt absurdly comforted to be back in hyperspace, although there was no air outside to replenish the dwindling supply inside. "Are the spores gone from your chassis, Lizzie?"

"You are safe now, Jeff sir, for my outer scanners show that hyperspace has destroyed all the spores that landed on me."

Norby blinked. "Did you carry along any poods?"

"What are poods?" asked Lizzie.

"I mean spyers . . . that's not right. Something about that alien language that mixes me up. Or maybe it's because I was influenced by the Connector, which thinks in that language even if it doesn't talk out loud. Jeff—what am I trying to say?"

Frightened, Jeff grabbed Norby and established a telepathic link.

—Show me.

The picture that entered Jeff's mind was of a red, eight-legged animal. With it was a strange word he didn't recognize although he knew it didn't fit the animal but something vaguely like it. Something he'd never seen. "Norby, are you trying to ask Lizzie if she carried with her any of those spiders we saw in that wrong version of Manhattan?"

"That's right. Spiders."

"Certainly not," Lizzie said. "I have scanned my surfaces and I am clean."

Norby said, "Maybe I'm not thinking of the real spiders we saw. Maybe I'm thinking of the Connector's way of using a cyberspace search program."

"Do you feel that it's still looking for you?" asked Jeff.

"No. It isn't. Maybe I miss it."

"Norby!"

"Sorry, Jeff. It was an unusual experience, being part of the Connector and turning Computer Prime into a conscious being. If only there hadn't been such sadness . . ."

"What do you mean?"

"I don't know. I can't figure it out."

"Then don't try right now, Norby. We have to restore the right time line."

Lizzie said, "Will we go back to prevent Computer Prime from deflecting the Cretaceous asteroid?"

"Not exactly," said Norby.

"But why not?" asked Lizzie.

"We can't go to a time when we already exist."

"I do not understand."

By now Jeff was feeling faint. "It's a peculiarity of time travel, Lizzie. We can't go back to the Cretaceous in time to *prevent* the deflection of the asteroid because we were in Computer Prime before and during the crash. I don't know what we should do. . . . It's hard to think. . . . I'm seeing little red spooders—I mean spiders—in front of me."

"Stop talking, Jeff," Norby said. "You look awful."

Norby's domed hat seemed to spin around, and Jeff blacked out. When he was conscious again, he opened his eyes to a blue sky dotted with white clouds. The air smelled odd but after taking deep breaths he felt better. Then he saw that he was lying on sand, with Lizzie's headlight scanners gazing solicitously at him and Norby perched on her hood. There was lush vegetation in one direction, greenish water in the other.

"Where am I?"

"On a Late Permian beach," Norby said. "About two hundred and twenty million years back from our time. You won't have to worry about dinosaurs because they have not evolved yet, and this air has no lethal spores."

Jeff rubbed his head, trying to remember. "Didn't the Permian have some rather large animals . . . ?"

As if answering Jeff, an animal as big as Lizzie waddled out of the vegetation bordering the sand. It had a heavy body, a broad, knobby head, and small stupid eyes that were gazing—meditatively, Jeff thought—at Lizzie.

Jeff scrambled to his feet. "What is that?"

"A pareiasaur called Scutosaurus," Norby said in his best teaching voice. "You learned vertebrate history at the Academy, but being human, you have forgotton most of it. Pareiasaurs were early reptiles, but don't worry, this one is vegetarian, so it's probably after that seaweed Lizzie landed on. It's low tide here and . . ."

Jeff interrupted. "What if it thinks I'm a new vegetable? And those creatures eating shelled things down there in the shallows are *not* vegetarians."

"Those are merely some of the big amphibians that the new reptiles of this time will eventually displace. This is a good opportunity for you to observe Permian animal life, Jeff."

Another creature trotted toward Lizzie from the opposite end of the beach. As big as Scutosaurus, this animal had legs that were more efficiently located under the body instead of jutting to the side. Jeff noticed that its pointed teeth were definitely on display.

Scutosaurus saw the newcomer, bellowed, and lowered its head like a bull ready for battle.

Jeff hopped into Lizzie, shutting the windows but leaving the roof panel open for air. "I'll observe Permian life from inside, thank you. I don't like the looks of what's arriving."

Norby joined Jeff and closed Lizzie's doors. "The animal that's coming is a Therapsid, a mammal-like reptile. Your distant ancestors, Jeff."

"It looks carnivorous . . . and hungry."

"Don't worry, Jeff. We can cope. Do your thing, Lizzie."

"Fear not, kind Jeff sir. Before you awoke I had already frightened away another of those therapsids."

Manhattan taxis are well equipped for intimidating other taxis in heavy air traffic. Lizzie honked her horn.

Both the carnivorous reptile and the distant carnivorous

amphibians paused in what they were doing. When Lizzie honked again, they retreated until almost out of sight.

The Scutosaurus did not retreat at all. It gave another, softer bellow and lumbered toward Lizzie, drooling a little, a glint in its beady eyes.

"Jeff sir, the Scutosaurus is nuzzling my rear end!"

"Whatever you do," Jeff said carefully, "don't honk or it will be sure you're a new mate. Just go up on antigrav, very slowly, so we won't hurt it."

As Lizzie rose into the air, the Scutosaurus made sad hooting noises until Lizzie was out of reach. Then it grunted and went back into the greenery.

Jeff sighed and shut the roof panel. "I've recovered from lack of air, and I think we should leave the Permian period before we do something that could change evolution."

As usual, Norby said, "Don't worry, Jeff. We're quite safe up here, where nothing bigger than insects can reach us because birds and flying reptiles have not evolved yet, so let Lizzie fill up with nice clean air."

Norby opened the windows and something as long as Jeff's foot flew into the taxi, banged into Jeff's forehead, dropped something on Jeff's lap, and whizzed out the other window.

"Don't worry, Jeff, that was only a small member of the order Mecoptera."

Jeff closed the windows again. "It was a *big* insect!"

"I know, Jeff, but the little scorpion flies of our time don't bite or sting humans. Probably this larger Permian scorpion fly is completely harmless."

"It dropped a dead cockroach on me. The biggest cockroach I've ever seen!"

"Undoubtedly the gift it was carrying to a prospective mate, who won't receive it because you got in the way, Jeff." Norby lowered a window and threw the cockroach out.

"Norby, I do not like being hit by huge insects and . . . what is that noise?"

It sounded like a hundred thunderstorms at once. Jeff

peered through Lizzie's windows as she hung over the beach. "That cloud in the distance can't be a nuclear bomb explosion, can it?"

"It's only a volcano, Jeff," Norby said. "I told you it's late Permian. But again you no doubt have forgotten . . ."

"It's coming back to me. At the start of the Permian period, there was one global continent, Pangea. During the next hundred million years or so, Pangea slowly moved around and split up, causing lots of flooding, volcanoes, dust, acid rain, poisonous gases polluting the atmosphere. . . ."

"What is the matter, Jeff sir? You suddenly sound unhappy."

"I am, Lizzie. I've just remembered that by the time this Permian period ended, ninety percent of animal life was extinct."

Norby waved his two-way hand. "Correct. The end of the Permian period was worse than a hundred and fifty-five million years later at the end of the Cretaceous period, when the asteroid hit—or should have hit, on the proper time line."

"I do not feel safe here!" Lizzie said with a quaver. "I do not like all these extinctions."

"First Jeff should replenish his energy with food."

Jeff ground his teeth. "How do you expect me to have an appetite when that volcano is belching out clouds? I do *not* want to be part of the Permian extinctions."

"Which took at least a million years and have not started quite yet. You have time to watch the volcano while you're eating your lunch."

Although it was good to be full, rested, and no longer oxygen starved, Jeff was relieved when Norby connected himself to Lizzie's engine and sent the taxi back into hyperspace.

Jeff tried to tell himself that if they corrected the past then they could return to their own era at almost the same time that they left. Telling himself was useless; it still felt as if they were wasting time in the past and ought to hurry.

86

"Let's get going, Norby. We must restore the future and we must rescue Computer Prime—and Garc. I'm beginning to think of him not as a villain but as the victim of that Connector."

"Victim is the word," Norby said, his head sinking lower into his barrel. "I've been under the influence of that Connector ring, and I know it's a powerful alien device that can make humans and robots do what it wants."

"Whether or not Garc is a villain or victim," Lizzie said, "I am willing to move on to the Cretaceous to do battle with the Connector. I want my own Manhattan to exist. I want my human passenger to feel safe. The air tank installed by our Rembrandt does not work properly."

"It's more likely that the Others use less oxygen in their metabolism than humans do," Norby said. "It also didn't help that you were upset, Jeff, because your emotions made you breathe more rapidly. Do try to control yourself."

"Control myself! When we have to go back to a dangerous time to try controlling an uncontrollable Connector?"

Norby flung up both arms, narrowly missing Jeff's head. "I admit that it's tricky. And the trickiest part is for me to get us back to the Cretaceous at almost the exact moment we left it."

A new thought struck Jeff. "It seems to me that we'll have two Connectors to cope with, the original that's in the alien ship, and the version of it that went through time and was found by Garc and brought back to the Cretaceous."

"I don't know, Jeff," Norby said. "Maybe. Maybe not. We'll have to play it by ear."

"You don't have an ear."

"I like the anatomical expressions of Basic Terran."

Lizzie quivered and a second later, they were out of hyperspace. Until the taxi's windows polarized, Jeff was almost blinded by the intensity of sunlight.

He turned to look out the windows on the other side and saw Earth in the distance, incredibly beautiful.

"Seems a shame to put that asteroid back on track," Jeff said. "Think of the devastation. . . ."

Norby said, "Remember that your mammalian ancestors won't have a chance if that asteroid ahead of us doesn't land."

"The asteroid is so big!" Lizzie exclaimed.

Jeff squinted in that direction. "Gosh, how fantastic! The asteroid is bigger than the scientists estimated, and there's Computer Prime stuck right into it. You were right, Norby. We hit the asteroid, not another spaceship, and both Computer Prime and the asteroid are now heading away from Earth."

"My taxi colleagues and the other vehicles are not on Computer Prime," Lizzie said. "They seem to be hovering aimlessly in space, as if they did not know what to do. And I can see in the distance a strange object like a ball with spokes on it. Is that the alien ship you encountered when you first went to the Cretaceous in *The Hopeful*?"

"That it is, Lizzie," said Jeff. "Norby, I think Computer Prime's propulsion system is too weak to move that big an asteroid back on course."

"Then we'll have to use the power of the Connector. Lizzie, take us into Computer Prime."

"It will be dangerous for you, Norby."

"There is no other choice."

14

The Secret of Garc the Great

As Lizzie flew toward Computer Prime, Jeff saw that its forward end had not penetrated far into the asteroid. And what an asteroid! It looked ten times the size of Computer Prime.

"Norby, I think it's more than the ten kilometers long that our scientists estimated."

"Much bigger. I think that confirms the theory that the Cretaceous asteroid split up as it entered Earth's atmosphere, one chunk landing at an angle on the Yucatan Peninsula, where evidence . . . what's the matter, Lizzie?"

"My colleagues. They are calling to me. They do not know how they came to be so far above Earth, and they do not know what to do. When the Connector tied them to Computer Prime, it must have canceled their computer recording."

"Tell them to follow us and wait outside Computer Prime."

Under any other circumstances, Jeff would have been amused to see all those Manhattan taxis floundering around, along with ungainly garbage scows and trucks and floating computer brain components, but he was too worried. "How are we ever going to make that enormous asteroid turn back, split, and land exactly where it did before?"

"I don't know. The original coordinates for the asteroid's trajectory will be in the alien ship."

"Which is firing at us, Jeff sir," Lizzie announced.

The flashes coming from the alien ship seemed bigger than they had before, thought Jeff, but that was because the ship was closer. Since sound does not travel through space, the danger was accompanied by a silence that somehow made the menace not quite real.

But it was real. A flash hit Lizzie and she screamed, "Hey, that hurt!"

"You are programmed to feel pain?" Jeff asked.

"All taxis feel pain when something hits us. How else would my more stupid colleagues be careful to avoid collisions?"

"Norby, open Computer Prime's airlock so Lizzie can get inside. Hurry!"

"It won't open. Garc must have changed the code. Hang on."

"Do you think you should risk—"

But it was too late. Norby had jumped them all into hyperspace and out again into the control room of Computer Prime.

"That was masterfully done, if I do say so myself," Norby said. "Computer Prime's hull is so thick that I doubt if the alien ship can damage it much. The energy arrows it was shooting at us could only bollix up relatively unshielded computer systems like Lizzie's."

Jeff opened the door and got out. Garc was lying on the control room floor. When Jeff reached down to turn Garc over, he saw that Garc was crying.

"You wicked, wicked person!" Garc jumped to his feet and began hitting Jeff.

"Stop it, Garc!" He didn't stop, but Jeff had longer, stronger arms and succeeded in pushing Garc away. "That's enough. Sit on the floor and don't move."

"We hit something and you left me," Garc wailed, sitting down. "Then the Connector left me, and then Computer Prime wasn't a person anymore, wasn't my friend, the being I created. You must have stolen the Connector and I want it back!"

"We didn't steal your blasted Connector," Jeff said. "It must have disappeared, because it already exists in this time, in the alien ship."

"What alien ship?"

"There in the viewscreen, coming at us."

"Must be a weather balloon or holov satellite."

"Garc, it is an alien enemy, and we are sixty-five million years in the past!"

Garc sniffed. "I don't believe in time travel."

"Computer Prime has already told you that we certainly have time traveled."

"I've decided that Computer Prime was under the influence of the Connector, so it can't be relied on. If you don't have the Connector, go away and leave me alone. I don't like people. I like machines. Just leave your taxi and your robot with me. They are needed as part of Computer Prime's larger self, the one that is conscious."

"I don't have time to argue with you, Garc," Jeff said, sitting in the command chair. One of the viewscreens showed that Computer Prime's nose was still against the asteroid. "Norby, we have to do what we can. Turn on the engine."

The little robot hopped to the control panel and plugged in. "It works. We're backing . . . uh-oh. I've made Computer Prime break loose instead of pulling the asteroid back."

"Can you get Computer Prime into orbit around Earth?"

"Done. But that doesn't help move the asteroid, Jeff."

"I know, but . . . Norby, the alien ship is getting closer."

"I see it. I can now sense that the Connector is inside it. You were right, Jeff. Because the Connector can't be in two places at once, the one we brought back had to disappear. Only the original remains, in the alien ship."

"Would that ship have the power to move the asteroid?"

"I don't know, but even if it could, the Exile wants the asteroid to move away from Earth, not toward it. That's why we're being attacked, so we won't change what's been changed."

"Neither of you is making any sense," said Garc. "I want to go home. I want my old ship back. . . . No, I want the Connector back. The Connector was the only thing that ever made me feel it needed me!"

Lizzie rolled closer to Jeff. "Kind human sir—as opposed to the unkind human sir who is yelling at us—I suggest that I be the one to go to the alien ship and try to retrieve the Connector. I know how to get inside it."

"How can you know that? When we were in the dinosaurs' city, we could only look at the ship in that pit."

"Somehow the different Rembrandt gave me the entry code."

Norby said, "Give it to me, Lizzie."

"No, Norby," Lizzie said. "You are more subject to the influence of the Connector than I am."

Norby got inside the taxi. "Stop mothering me, Lizzie. Come along, Jeff. I'll hyperjump us right against the alien ship's airlock. I don't dare jump inside the ship because I don't know what it's like."

Jeff got in but kept the door open. "Leave, Norby. Lizzie and I will go alone."

"I'm staying, Jeff. Don't you realize that the Connector is not controlling me, and probably won't? It doesn't need to, because the Connector has accomplished its purpose—to keep Earth safe for the Exile, and for the dinosaurs."

"Then how will we ever . . ."

"We'll play it—"

"By ear. You are the stubbornnest robot in the Galaxy."

"But I'm yours, Jeff. You are my responsibility."

"You are not going without me!" Garc yelled, getting in Lizzie's front seat. "If you're going for the Connector, so am I, because it belongs to me. My ship's metal detectors found it floating in the Oort Cloud. It's mine by right of discovery."

"Since we'll need to replace the Connector, can you pinpoint the exact location again?" asked Jeff.

Garc's smile disappeared. "Don't want to discuss that."

"Doesn't your ship's computer monitor all locations?"

"Well, er . . . naw. Too old."

Jeff touched Norby.

—This is disastrous. Even if we successfully steal the Connector and move the asteroid, we've got to put it where Garc is going to find it, in our time, or things won't be the same, and time won't be put right, and Fargo and Albany and Admiral Yobo will never exist. . . .

—Courage, Jeff. We'll have to unravel the time travel paradoxes as they come along.

—Oh, fine. The history of the world is at stake and we're going to fix it up without knowing how.

Lizzie swayed impatiently. "Are we ready to go?"

"Garc," Jeff said, "get out of Lizzie."

Norby said, "Maybe he should stay."

"He's a troublemaker!"

"I am not!" Garc said. "I am just a gar—I mean, I'm basically a good person."

"Gar what?" asked Jeff.

"Don't want to tell. Are you going to let me go with you?"

Lizzie said, "Jeff sir, I think Norby is right to let the human Garc go with us. He knows the Connector better than you or I—and it knows him. It may be more easily stolen by him than by you."

Jeff touched Norby.

—Lizzie hasn't grasped the fact that the Connector in the alien ship must be the original, which has not yet gone into history and been found by Garc. Why do *you* want me to take Garc along?

—Do you think robots can have intuition, Jeff?

—I guess if any robot can, mine does. Are you saying you suspect that it might be a good idea to take Garc along but you don't know why?

—That's it, Jeff. Besides, Garc is so noisy and nasty that he could be somewhat of a, um . . .

—Distraction?

—Exactly.

Jeff looked at Garc, cowering in the corner of the taxi. "All right, Garc, you can go with us on one condition. Tell us what 'gar' means."

"What'll you do to me if I don't tell?"

"I will knock you out and let you sleep on the floor of Computer Prime until we get back."

Garc seemed to be studying the size of Jeff's fists. "I am Garc the Great."

"Uh-huh. We're wasting time, and the asteroid is getting farther away. I'm going to knock you out—"

"My name is Yaskill Ames."

"Ames?" Norby asked. "Sounds familiar. My first owner, MacGillicuddy, used to talk about a Yarbo Ames."

"My father. Our family is an ancient line of—"

"Of what?" Jeff asked, aching to shake Garc.

"Space Garbage Collectors. Get it—Gar-Co?"

"Norby, take us to the alien ship before I hit this great garbage collector."

15

The Alien Ship

With Jeff, Garc, and Norby inside, Lizzie hovered just outside the alien ship's airlock. Jeff tried to be calm, but it was unnerving to see that the other taxis were now flitting around the alien ship like bees attracted to a strange flower. One by one, they became impaled on its spokes.

"Kind sirs," Lizzie said with a tinny quaver in her voice. "I do not like what is happening to my colleagues."

"Must be the Connector," Norby said, "yet I don't feel any pull from it. Do you, Lizzie?"

"Not yet."

"Then we must go on," Jeff said. "Lizzie, the airlock looks plenty big enough for you. While you're flying in, occupy your mind with something so you'll have some resistance to the Connector's influence, as you did before."

"I have decided to count and describe all the trees in Central Park that I have ever seen. There are a good many. What will you use to occupy your mind, Norby?"

"I hardly need . . . well, maybe I do. I will correlate the grammar of the Others' language with that of Terran Basic and its component languages. Since there is very little correlation, the effort may serve to confuse the Connector. I should have thought of such a ruse after Fargo's wedding, but the Connector took me by surprise."

"Okay," Jeff said. "Now that you two are prepared, let's go inside. Use the code, Lizzie."

"I hope we find the Connector," said Garc, who had begged Jeff to continue using that name instead of Yaskill Ames.

The airlock opened and Lizzie flew in. "The air coming into

95

the airlock is breathable by humans, but do not open my windows. If anything goes wrong, you will be safer inside me."

"I want to get out," Garc said, bobbing up and down on the front seat.

"Human Garc, I am programmed to protect my passengers, and you are now one, here to help us accomplish an important task. You are, however, not a passenger I would choose to pick up if you were hailing a taxi in Manhattan."

"Nobody likes me," Garc mumbled.

Jeff glared at him. "Maybe that's because you don't seem to like anybody—human or machine."

"I love Computer Prime. Thanks to me, Computer Prime became a person, until you took the Connector from me."

"I've told you that I didn't take it, Garc. The Connector vanished when we entered this time zone—"

"I don't believe you! It's a plot to get my property!"

"Can't you understand that you have changed history, and that you and I are the only humans alive—"

"Nonsense."

Jeff gave up, grateful when Garc lapsed into sulky silence.

The inner end of the airlock dilated.

Lizzie announced, "I regret to inform you that I am being pulled inside by some sort of tractor beam, which I cannot stop."

"Don't worry about it, Lizzie," said Norby. "We have to go in anyway."

There was no entrance hall. Lizzie was drawn directly into a gigantic, machine-lined room, evidently the entire inside of the ball-shaped ship.

"There is no antigrav here, kind sirs. I am floating."

So was the alien positioned at the largest of six computer-studded, triangular control boards. The Exile was a bright, iridescent green with lighter green spokes, and she—Jeff remembered that the second Rembrandt had called her "she"—was ball-shaped, just like her own ship.

The control boards were not on the walls and they did not

float. Their broad ends were fixed to the circular wall by long wires. Their pointed ends were fixed to each other by shorter wires that met in the center of the control room.

"There's my Connector!" shouted Garc, pointing to the Connector. Its gleaming gold circle rested on the exact center where the shorter wires met.

One of the Exile's spokes was elongated, touching the large control board. Another, on the opposite side of the spherical body, was elongated much more, its tip gently but firmly touching the Connector.

"That creature could not possibly get around in Earth's gravity," Jeff said. "Unless she flies."

"Perhaps she has her own built-in antigrav for use on planets," Norby said.

"Look, kind sirs, the anatomy of that creature is changing, and I do not like it!"

Two of the creature's other spokes swelled at their ends like bursting buds. Each bud opened to a purple eye—large, lustrous, and fixed on Lizzie.

Jeff tried to sound calm. "We have her attention, Norby. You know the alien language, so use it to let her know who we are and why we are here."

"Okay. I'll give you the translation telepathically while I speak it to the alien."

—Exile, listen to me. We are time travelers who have made a terrible mistake and you must help us undo it or the consequences will be terr . . .

Two more of the alien's green spokes turned to Lizzie, vibrating. A glowing energy packet flashed out.

Jeff felt it as a painful prickling down his spine, while Garc exclaimed, "Ow!"

Lizzie said, "Please make it stop that, Jeff sir. It not only hurts, but I am afraid that the Connector will snare me into the machinery of this ship."

—Norby, are you being affected by the Connector?

—The energy bolts feel awful, but I am not succumbing to

its influence. I think it's because I'm touching you, Jeff, and you are my owner.

—And your friend.

—You are protecting me from the Connector.

Out loud, Norby said, "Lizzie, be sure that your brain is mostly occupied with those trees you were talking about."

"Yes, Norby. I will try to be brave even if this alien hurts me."

In a tinnier voice, Norby tried to continue talking to the alien.

—Exile, please listen. We live sixty-five million years from now, but by coming here and stopping the asteroid from hitting the planet below, we have changed history—

This time, the energy bolt was so strong that Jeff shut his eyes and gritted his teeth in pain. When he opened his eyes, he saw that Norby's head was shut inside his barrel.

"Norby!"

Norby's hat elevated slightly until the tops of his eyes showed above the barrel's brim. "Sorry, Jeff. That was a tough one. We can't take much more of this attack. I mean, I can't. It agitates both my emotive and cognitive circuits."

Garc's sharp elbow nudged Jeff. "Why are you playing with spiked balloons? I want my Connector."

"Shut up, Garc. Norby, can't you explain to the Exile— Lizzie, duck or something!"

The taxi dipped down and the next energy bolt missed.

"Not very sophisticated weapons. No guidance system," Norby muttered. "Lizzie, can you fly over to the Connector?"

"Of course I can. Must I?"

"Yes. I have a theory. To check it out, you must extend your claw and remove the Connector."

"I will try, Norby, but you must protect yourself by concentrating on that grammar problem or something. And something more . . . I should have thought of this before, but it is not a usual problem in a Manhattan taxi's life."

"What are you talking about?" asked Norby.

A section of Lizzie's back floor popped open. Jeff quickly drew up his legs because something shot out of the opening. It was gray and circular and expanding.

"I do not use my wheels except on land," Lizzie said, "and they are quite strongly built. Nevertheless, I do have a spare wheel, expandable and made of a genuine biological material called rubber."

Norby jiggled. "Lizzie, you are wasting time!"

"Norby, I am responsible for the welfare of my passengers and you are badly affected by the attack of that creature. Since the bolts have an electrical nature, I suggest that you sit yourself on my spare."

"Do it, Norby," Jeff urged. "I read that rubber does not conduct electricity. Remember not to touch any of Lizzie's chassis when the bolt—Here it comes again!"

The taxi rocked, but Lizzie said, "I will not be defeated." She flew in the direction of the Connector, but had not quite arrived when she was hit again and stopped short.

This time Jeff felt as if electrical worms were crawling over his skin and stinging him. He had a hard time trying to catch his breath.

"It worked, Lizzie," Norby said. "I didn't feel anything."

"I hurt," Garc moaned. "I must be having a terrible nightmare and can't wake up."

"You're awake," Jeff said sourly.

"This nightmare will stop if I get what I want," Garc said.

"Stop, Garc, don't open the door!"

Garc paid no attention. He pushed himself away from Lizzie and toward the Connector like an Olympic swimmer leaving the edge of a pool. He was hit by a bolt, but kept on.

"My Connector!" Garc plucked it from its resting place.

Instantly, the inside of the alien ship went dark. When Lizzie turned on her headlights, Jeff saw that the Exile was hovering over Garc, but not touching him, her spokes beating like huge cilia.

"Is she saying anything?" Jeff asked Norby.

"No. I sense . . . terror."

"I know I am terrified," Lizzie said. "Perhaps you are merely tuning in to my emotive circuits, Norby."

"I don't think I am."

Jeff wondered why he no longer felt any electrical bolts. Perhaps they were all aimed at Garc. He opened Lizzie's window and shouted, "Are you all right, Garc? Is the alien causing you any pain?"

At first Garc grinned like a gray-bearded demon, but then he gave Jeff a venomous look. "Hah! You don't think I've caught on. I know perfectly well that there is no alien here."

"There certainly is, and you and I are lucky that we can breathe the alien's air. Now bring the Connector back—"

"I won't, because I know you're a spy, creating holographic illusions to persuade me to surrender the Connector to Space Command. They'll take the Connector apart and duplicate it. Then everyone will have its power except me."

"The alien is real, and may kill us before we can use the Connector to restore the time line. Get back in the taxi!"

Norby said softly, "Now that the Exile isn't touching the Connector, she's stopped shooting electrical bolts."

Jeff whispered back, "If the Connector gives that sort of power, Garc has it now, and he can't be trusted."

"Most unpleasant," Lizzie said. "I must do something about the problem." Abruptly she wrenched the Connector from Garc's hands with her extensible hook.

"Give it back!" Garc screeched in rage.

Lizzie opened her roof and dropped the Connector inside. It plunged down on Jeff's head.

"Take it off, Jeff!" Norby exclaimed.

"I can't! It's stuck as if it were glued to my head."

"It shrank to fit your head, but its mass is the same because it's thicker than it was before. It looks like a golden crown on you, Jeff. Is it hurting you?"

"No, it doesn't hurt. It just . . . feels strange."

"I'll get rid of it," said Norby, reaching out.

"No! You must not risk any contact with the Connector."

Garc was trying to swim through the air toward Lizzie, who closed her windows and roof. "I know I am supposed to accept passengers, but he is a villain. I will not let him in."

Garc kicked Lizzie's doors. "Give me the Connector!" he fumed, hanging in the gravityless air of the alien ship.

"Norby," Lizzie said in a worried tone, "Jeff looks sick."

"He needs help, Lizzie. We must leave."

"But Norby . . . oops! Must you transfer me to hyperspace so abruptly and—Oh! Now we're back in Computer Prime and we've left Garc in the alien ship!"

"As I intended. Jeff, are you any better? Jeff?"

"Who?"

"Jeff, pay attention! Are you feeling any better?"

"Jeff sir, Norby brought us back to Computer Prime."

Computer . . . Norby . . . Who is Norby? Who am I?

16

Making the Plunge

—Seeing . . . hearing . . . someone angry . . . shaking . . .

"Jeff, answer me!"

"Norby, Jeff ordered you not to touch him, and I fear that shaking him like that will not restore his consciousness."

"Lizzie, he's controlled by the Connector. With Garc and the Exile in the alien ship, I can concentrate here on touching Jeff and reaching his mind."

"I advise against it. You and he could both be taken over."

"Wait, Lizzie."

—Jeff, listen with your mind.

—Do not want touch . . . push bothersome object . . . leave this machine.

"Norby, I told you not to touch Jeff. Are you damaged?"

"No, but Jeff's heading for Computer Prime's control board."

—Walking . . . strange sensation. Sitting . . . odd.

"Norby, maybe you shouldn't get out."

"Jeff, this is Norby. Listen to me—"

"Silence, robot! I understand your language now and I am able to speak aloud through this being."

"Norby, the Connector spoke to you in Jeff's voice. How come it never spoke through Garc?"

"Because Jeff is telepathic, thanks to me, and the Connector can make closer contact with him. Connector, release Jeff!"

"I am the Connector. The Exile and I will change and teach the creatures of the planet below. I cannot prolong the Exile's life, but by diverting the asteroid, I have made it possible for her civilization to continue here."

"Jeff, you're trapped by the Connector, but you must make it listen to the truth—that it was useless to divert the asteroid and save the dinosaurs."

Lizzie said, "He is not listening. Why are you and I not overpowered by the Connector now? Both of us were before."

"That might be Jeff's doing, and it gives me hope. Lizzie, I must get closer to Jeff and try again to bypass the Connector."

"Robot, if you keep touching, I will control you, too."

"Norby? Oh, dear, he's in Jeff's arms, all closed up! I'm alone with this monster of a Connector. . . . Listen, Mr. Connector, this is Lizzie the taxi speaking. Today you made a different future possible, but in it, the dinosaurs killed themselves off."

"You are incorrect, taxi. I took no such information from Computer Prime's data banks."

"Computer Prime was not there. Read the memories of Jeff and Norby, who were there."

"I have shut out the babbling of their complicated minds to make it easier to use their mental energy."

"Connector, I am only a simple taxi. There—I am touching you with my hook so you can see the information in pictures."

"I am being touched. . . . I am Connector. . . . Connector-Jeff, who likes Lizzie . . . images, memories of the future . . ."

"You see the pictures, Connector? In the future, the city of the dinosaurs will be in ruins."

"It cannot . . . must not be. On the other time line, my Exile left me in the cloud of comets at the edge of this solar system, with instructions to wait for someone capable of time travel. Her ship went on, and I sensed her death. I have obeyed her commands and come back to this time period to save her."

"Mistakes. You have the truth, Connector, so please admit to yourself that the civilization of the Exile cannot be continued with the dinosaurs."

"Sadness . . . hopelessness."

"Nothing is ever totally hopeless," said Lizzie, flashing her headlights. "Jeff! This is Lizzie! You know me, and you know you are human and you know my information is true."

—Conscious . . . I . . . am . . . Jeff . . . Norby! Leave!

"Well, at least you have released Norby, Connector."

"Jeff did it, Lizzie. He's trying to regain control."

—Read my memories, Connector. I am Jeff Wells, and I tell you the truth.

"Jeff, are you back?"

"Yes, Norby." Jeff was suddenly able to remove the Connector and hold it in his hands. The Connector could no longer talk but he could still hear it in his mind, and he knew that the Connector could hear him.

"Connector, I know that you were only trying to do your job, and it isn't your fault that it turned out to be a mistake."

—I am an artificial intelligence, like your robot's, but without his mobility and talents. My talent is to connect minds and control their power, in the service of those who made me. The Exile is the last survivor. She will die with no way to pass on her knowledge, her history.

"Connector, I am holding you and I know you can hear what I say and also read my mind. On the correct time line, my civilization still lasts."

—I know.

"See these other images in my mind. A possibility?"

—Perhaps. If the Exile is willing. Her species is more emotional than yours.

Jeff was glad Norby couldn't hear that. "Okay, but we must push the asteroid back on course before it gets farther away."

Lizzie had left Computer Prime to join her taxi colleagues hovering in space outside.

"Jeff sir," she said by intercom, "we vehicles are ready to help Computer Prime push the asteroid into the right trajectory for hitting Earth. Are you and Norby achieving a telepathic link with the Connector and Computer Prime's brain?"

"We're trying, Lizzie," Jeff said. Holding the Connector, Jeff touched Norby, at Computer Prime's control board, and began to feel as if he might at any moment have a nasty headache.

"Norby, can we be certain that we'll push the asteroid into the right trajectory? And its got to hit at an angle—that's what caused all the fires to start in North America."

"From the Connector's data, we know approximately the way the asteroid was heading at the time Computer Prime hit it."

"It seems so uncertain, and what if . . ."

Norby jiggled in exasperation. "Jeff, your worries are interfering. If we're going to have enough power to do this job, you must concentrate!"

"But this four-way telepathic link is so weird—you and I and Computer Prime's brain, and that alien Connector . . ."

"Concentrate, Jeff!"

"It's hard. . . . I can't . . ." As Jeff said it, he suddenly felt a surge of reaction that was not human. Could it be from . . . Computer Prime? "Norby! Computer Prime wants to shut itself off!"

"I know. I'm trying to cope. Computer Prime, you're now a conscious being with emotive reactions and you are afraid, but you must help us before we can return to our own time."

Was Computer Prime relieved? Jeff could not tell. He worried . . . or was it the Connector?

Norby said, "Jeff, your emotions are overpowering the rest of us. Please try singing. It calms Fargo, and your baritone hardly ever cracks these days. While you sing, the Connector and I and Computer Prime will work on the asteroid."

Jeff searched through his memory for a suitable song, but the one that came up was doggerel, and the words that came out were not those he remembered, but a peculiar mixture.

"Pick a peck of peopled planets," said the Spooder to the Flur,
"I'll toss you moons and whuppence or a double im and ur."
Said the Flur all griv and iggy to the Spooder yning there,

*"Why don't both of us go ukling since there's quite enough to
  share."*

Jeff could hear Norby laughing, but he went on singing the
strange song, ending up with:

*So for tasty gor de oozin fifty spaceships did delight,
And they gossed and wunched and borbyrd with galactic
   appetite.*

The link was suddenly broken, and Jeff could hear Lizzie
yelling through her intercom.

"Jeff sir! Norby! Save yourselves—"

Staring at Computer Prime's viewscreen, Jeff thought Earth
looked as if it were an enormous, ball-shaped alien, pulling to
itself whatever was near.

"—because the asteroid is now heading for Earth, and so
are you in Computer Prime!"

"Lizzie's right, Norby, Computer Prime's stuck in the asteroid and we'll crash with it. Get us loose."

He turned around, but Norby was not there, and neither
was the Connector.

"Lizzie, can you hear me? Norby's disappeared with the
Connector. I'm at the control board, trying to—"

"Hurry, Jeff sir!"

"I've detached Computer Prime from the asteroid, but I
can't seem to bring up enough power to go back into a safe
orbit."

"Jeff sir, inside Computer Prime you are still heading for
impact, but do not fear. We Manhattan taxis are strong."

He heard a faint crunch as several taxis and garbage scows
hit the planetward side of Computer Prime a little too hard.

They're only taxis and garbage scows, he thought. Where is
Norby? If he doesn't come back I'll be part of the cataclysm
that closed the Cretaceous period. Me and the dinosaurs.

But little by little, the space between Computer Prime and

Earth widened, while Jeff watched the asteroid break in two in the atmosphere, the pieces glowing red as their bright paths curved down. When they hit Earth, great clouds billowed up, and soon there were tremendous flashes of light as if huge volcanoes had been triggered into erupting.

The control room door burst open and Lizzie flew in. "Jeff sir, you are in a stable orbit around Earth. You are safe."

"Thanks, Lizzie, but without Norby, I'll have to spend my life here. Take me over to the alien ship."

"That is a bad idea, Jeff sir. The Exile has probably killed Garc and may kill you, and . . . well, hello, Norby. Dropping by, now that the excitement is over? Where have you been, you naughty robot?"

"Busy. Sorry to have left abruptly, but the Connector insisted it had to investigate something."

Jeff was appalled. "You left the Connector somewhere?"

"Uh-huh. Now let me work. You can listen in, Jeff." As Norby tied in to Computer Prime, Jeff touched him, and was instantly aware of telepathic conversation.

—Norby, like the Connector, you make me conscious, aware of myself . . . and unhappy. I want only to be vaguely aware of being a good library. I beg you to return me to that.

—Right now.

Jeff was about to object, when Computer Prime shivered, the viewscreen went gray, and then showed a blackness that was filled with objects.

Stars—and spaceships!

17

Getting Help

—You are home, Computer Prime. The Connector is gone, and when I withdraw, I will no longer be part of you. You will stop being conscious.

—Norby, I wish only to be rid of consciousness. It is suitable for robots like you and Lizzie, and for sentient organics like your Jeff. My function is to accumulate, correlate, and store data—and that is what I wish to do, without thinking and worrying about it. Thank you and farewell.

—Good-bye, Computer Prime.

Norby's antennae withdrew from Computer Prime's control board, ending the telepathic conversation of one machine to another.

"Are we really back in our own time?" asked Jeff.

"You can see the admiral's fleet, can't you? I want you to know that I have outdone myself. I've returned Computer Prime to the time shortly after the moment when we left."

"How shortly? And did we leave Lizzie and the other vehicles back in the Cretaceous?"

"No. Look again in the viewscreen, Jeff. There's Lizzie trying to herd her colleagues together. They must have been touching Computer Prime when I brought us back here."

"That's good. Hey, something just lit up on the board."

"Message signal." Norby touched a switch and Admiral Yobo's bass voice boomed out.

"Cadet! Answer me!"

"Admiral Yobo? Is everything all right?"

"You tell me, Jeff. After you went into Computer Prime—and I'd like to know how the classified entry code was broken—all communication with you stopped. Fargo was unable to enter, so we started trying to break down Computer Prime's defenses and got that insolent message from Garc. Where is he?"

"I'm not exactly sure, Admiral. Except that right now he is definitely not inside Computer Prime."

"I suppose he escaped when Computer Prime vibrated," Yobo said, with a slight emphasis on the word *vibrated*. Jeff knew that Yobo knew what had happened—that Computer Prime had actually left that time and space.

"Yes, Admiral. Garc left while Computer Prime vibrated."

"Everyone in the fleet is remarking about how odd Computer Prime looked, almost as if it were not there for a second."

Norby said telepathically—You see, only a second of their time has elapsed. I told you that I am a paragon of efficiency in time travel, Jeff.

—Sometimes.

"Cadet, are you listening?"

"Yes, sir. Is Computer Prime part of the Solarweb again?"

"It is, Cadet. Our computers are again linked with Computer Prime. Whatever Garc did has now been undone." Yobo sounded pleased and then, to Jeff's surprise, he switched to the language of the Others in order to speak one word, growled as if he were clearing his throat.

"Permanently?"

Jeff looked at Norby.

"Yes, sir," Norby said.

Another voice broke in. "Little brother, in my space suit I was a lot closer to Computer Prime than the fleet was so I had a better view of its—ah—vibration. Perhaps we'd better discuss this whole thing later?"

"Yes, Fargo. Go back inside Jonesy and tell Albany that everything is okay."

"If that's true, we'll be off on our honeymoon. Will you be picking up Oola from you know where?"

109

"Yes. Enjoy yourself."

—Norby, the admiral and Fargo can't ask us about Computer Prime's travels, not with the fleet listening, so we'll tell them our adventures later. I'm going to send for Lizzie. You know what we must do.

—I know.

Aloud, Jeff said, "Admiral, I've got to use the—er—human facilities here, so you won't be hearing from me for a while. Please tell Lizzie to come inside Computer Prime. We'll go back to Earth in her."

"You will not go back to Earth, Cadet, for you are due at the Academy. You seem to have forgotton that you were only excused from classes to attend your brother's wedding."

"Yes, sir, Norby and I will return to the Academy. After I, that is . . ."

"Use the facilities. I understand, Cadet. Your reconverted taxi is on her way."

Norby sped through the long main corridor of Computer Prime, hauling Jeff to the entry hall. While Jeff went to use the washroom, Norby greeted Lizzie.

It seemed like a tremendous luxury to be able to pee, wash up, and have a cold glass of water. When he returned to the entry hall he found Norby inside Lizzie and arguing with her.

"You must obey orders, Lizzie!"

"Not when it will endanger my human passenger. Norby, it is not safe to go back to the Cretaceous period!"

Jeff got into the taxi. "Lizzie, we can't leave Garc in the alien ship, perhaps to be killed by the Exile. And I feel terrible about depriving the Exile of her Connector, because without it she can't fly her ship. It might go into the sun."

"The alien ship won't do that," Norby said. "I read her computer data banks and I know that the ship has fail-safe devices that keep it free from the gravity of any planet or star. Without the Connector, of course, the ship has no drive power, so it will undoubtedly drift out through the solar system."

"But it will never get to another solar system by the time the Exile and Garc die!" said Jeff.

"Jeff, they've been dead for sixty-five million years. Now don't look at me like that. The laws of robotics are still intact. I'm only trying to give you a perspective on it. I am willing to try to rescue them, if you can persuade this stubborn taxi to obey."

Lizzie said, irately, "In addition to the danger to you, Jeff sir, I fear that a rescue attempt will not be successful. If we try to rescue both Garc and the Exile, how will we carry them to safety? The Exile is too big to fit inside me, even if I were completely empty."

"I hadn't thought of that," said Norby. "I suppose I could ride on Lizzie's roof with the Exile, trying to keep her inside my personal field, but she's such a prickly being—"

Lizzie suddenly interrupted. "Admiral Yobo calling. Putting him on."

"Jeff, Norby, Lizzie—listen. I have just received a message that scavenging ships have found an alien vessel drifting near the Oort Cloud. Cadet, this alien ship is round with spokes all over it, which for some reason makes me think of our recent travels on our way to the wedding. Only this ship looks incredibly old."

"Is it open?"

"No, sealed up tight. The scavengers have been told by Space Command scientists that they must not attempt entry. Since there's only one transporter set up near the Oort Cloud, it will take a while for the scientists to get there with proper equipment for breaking into the ship. Do you understand, Cadet?"

"Yes, sir. We'll be going now, sir."

"Good luck again, Jeff. Yobo out."

"Hurry, Norby, we must go back to the Cretaceous and remove Garc from that ship, or the present-day scientists will find his body when they open it."

"First we must solve the problem of moving the Exile, if she's willing to be moved, and that's a good question—"

"Norby! Stop wasting time! Hurry, we must beat the scientists to the Exile's ship!"

"Jeff, with your soft heart, you want to rescue both the Exile and Garc, don't you?"

"You know I want to rescue them both, but I can't see how."

Another voice emerged from Lizzie's loudspeaker. "Join me. I can help you."

Norby gave a tinny chuckle and everything vanished outside Lizzie. The taxi was in the gray of hyperspace.

Lizzie said, "I cannot see anything, but my sensors say that I am against something metal."

"Welcome, Lizzie," Rembrandt's voice said. "The airlock is open. Come in."

"Forgive me for having continued to monitor your conversations in Lizzie," Rembrandt said when they had all assembled in the observation room of the Others' ship.

"I'm glad you did," Jeff said. "Stop that, Oola." The All-Purpose-Pet was so glad to see him that she kept trying to wash his face and neck.

Norby said, "You seem to have fed Oola well, Rembrandt. She's very fat."

"Indeed, but it is not fat—"

"Norby! Rembrandt!" Jeff yelled. "We haven't time to waste discussing Oola! This ship is big enough to transport the Exile, so I insist that we try to rescue her as well as Garc. I can't stand the idea of leaving her to die millions of years ago, and then her body being dissected by Federation scientists and probably put on display."

Lizzie said primly, "The Exile is—was—not at all a nice being."

"Lizzie!"

"Yes, Jeff sir, I know the laws of robotics, and I am willing to go with you, but I am programmed to care for *human* organics. It is my duty to point out again that even with the help of the Others, this mission may be very dangerous for you."

"Heard and understood," Jeff said. "Norby, join with Yib and take us to the Cretaceous—with your permission, Rembrandt."

"Go ahead, Norby. Yib is willing to go now that the Connector is no longer a threat. Norby, where did you take it?"

"Tell you later. Busy now." Norby attached himself to Yib and without even a tremor, the huge ship of the Others emerged into normal space, within a kilometer of the alien ship.

Earth was farther away than before, but Jeff could see the roiling clouds of disaster circling the planet. "Norby, how long has it been—here, I mean—since the asteroid struck?"

"I'm afraid that I was not so efficient this time. I think twenty-four hours have elapsed."

"Garc may be dead. Try again."

"There's a hycom message coming through," Rembrandt said, "but I do not understand the language."

"I do," Norby said, listening. "The Exile asks if we have come to destroy her or to help her." Norby spoke in the alien language, and then translated. "I just told her we're here to help so she must let our airlocks join and open to each other."

"Didn't you ask about Garc?" Jeff demanded.

"Of course not. If she's killed him and knows that we know him, she won't want to let us in, will she?"

Rembrandt smiled. "Logical reasoning, Norby."

The Exile spoke again and Norby translated. "She agrees to let us in. Here we go."

"Airlocks joined," said Rembrandt. "I am eager to meet this Exile from a different universe."

"You may change your mind," said Jeff.

18

Rescue

Lizzie insisted on taking Jeff and Rembrandt through the airlock into the alien ship. "You must stay inside me, kind sirs. I can seal myself in the event of danger to organics."

"I'll be more mobile if I sit on your hood," Norby said. "Without the Connector, the Exile probably can't harm me."

Jeff had to extract an eager Oola from Lizzie and put her onto the floor of the Others' observation room. "Oola, go sit on that cushion and don't move until we get back."

For once, Oola obeyed, but she started to howl when Jeff and Rembrandt entered the taxi (she usually turned into a hound when she was sad).

"We'll be back, Oola," Jeff said. He had no time to wonder why she looked so fat, because he was trying to think of how to persuade the Exile to leave her own ship and go with the Others.

With Norby on her hood, Lizzie made her way into the alien control room. It was so dark that Jeff could not find the Exile, much less Garc. When Lizzie turned on her headlights, Jeff saw that the Exile was as far from the airlock as possible.

"There is a human wedged into the space between two of the Exile's spokes," said Rembrandt. "If that is Garc, he does not look alive."

"Norby," Jeff said through Lizzie's loudspeaker, "tell the Exile to release Garc's body."

Before Norby had a chance to speak, the body stiffened, the head rose, and the mouth opened.

"What do you mean, 'body'? And I certainly do look alive. Did that Manhattan taxi bring food? I'm starving."

114

"Your compatriot Garc has not been killed," Rembrandt said in his own language. "I wish we could speak directly to the alien in her language."

"Norby," Jeff said, "help me communicate with the Exile. Try a mind link, translating back and forth as we speak. Lizzie, I can't open your door, and I want to get out."

"I have not released the door lock because I will take you to the Exile, Jeff sir. I do not trust that alien, but she will probably allow me near her. After all, everyone trusts Manhattan taxis, do they not?"

"I wouldn't say that," said Norby, winking at Jeff. "Be prepared to close up if Jeff and Rembrandt are in danger."

The Exile seemed to shrink back against the wall as they approached her, and she quivered when Norby grabbed one of her spokes and then stretched out his other arm to touch Jeff's hand.

Jeff tried not to let his fears show as he leaned out of Lizzie's window, holding Rembrandt with one hand and Norby by the other. Although it seemed as if the Exile were powerless without the Connector, Jeff felt as if any minute she would electrocute all of them.

Garc peered at the strange little chain of alien, robot, human, and Other, complete with taxi. "Just what do you idiots think you are doing?"

"We're trying to help," Jeff said.

"She'll poke you if you don't either stay away or get between the spokes, the way I did."

"Garc, we're trying to rescue you, but if you don't keep quiet we'll have second thoughts about it."

"I don't care, boy, and who's the three-eyed man?"

"If you value your life, Garc, shut up!"

There was a sudden silence, during which Jeff tried to organize his thoughts to speak telepathically.

—Exile, we have never meant you harm, yet in the past you have attacked us whenever we appeared. Please do not do that.

—You organics and your strange machines appeared without warning, and you have now stolen my Connector. Why should I not attack you? You deserve death.

"Amazing," muttered Rembrandt. "I can understand her."

"I think Norby's telepathy makes it possible," Jeff said. The Exile's words came through telepathically in Terran Basic, after only a tiny time lag, during which Norby was presumably translating. Jeff tried to continue.

—We want to help you, Exile. You must come with us.

—I do not believe you, two-eyes. You and that new three-eyed creature with you must have evil powers, for you can disappear and reappear. My name is Idge, and I am the last of my kind. I carry within me the knowledge of my species, and it is my duty to give it to trustworthy sentient beings, but I do not trust you.

—Idge, I am a human named Jeff Wells. With me in the vehicle named Lizzie is an organic being named Rembrandt. My robot Norby makes telepathic contact with you possible. He also has the capacities for hyperdrive and time travel. We come from sixty-five million planet years in the future.

—If you have hyperdrive, you must have entered this solar system from elsewhere in this universe, for time travel is impossible.

One of her spokes seemed to lengthen toward Jeff, who gulped and tried again.

—Idge, I can prove I'm from the far future, and that I have seen not only the real future where I was born, but also the false future created by your Connector.

—You speak nonsense.

"She's as bad as Garc," Norby said aloud, in the language of the Others. Rembrandt chuckled.

—Exile, listen to me. In the false future, I got data from your ship's memory banks, so I know that you came here from another universe, fleeing the destruction your species had caused in your own. I know that when two of your ships escaped to this universe, they fought and everyone but you died.

The Exile's green color paled, and her spokes trembled.

—Idge, when you arrived from your own universe, you landed in this solar system, near Earth, the planet below. Earth had no intelligent life, and an asteroid would soon devastate the life that did exist on it. You did not want to risk your ship in trying to change the direction of the asteroid, so you gave up.

—Stop! I do not want to listen.

—You must listen. I think you tried to invent the hyperdrive you wanted so badly, but by the time you were near the edge of this solar system, you realized that you would die in your ship, in intergalactic space. In the hope that intelligent life would eventually evolve in this solar system, you left the Connector to be found.

—I have not put these thoughts into the record.

—But on the other time line, you did, and they were read. The Connector was found and it brought us back to change history. When you saw that the asteroid was diverted away from Earth, you decided to bioengineer the dinosaurs, the planet's dominant life form, and transfer your knowledge to them.

—It would have been my way of ensuring that my species will contribute something to this universe.

"I'm getting tired of this," Garc shouted, squirming out from his seat between spokes. He pushed himself to Lizzie and hopped into her front seat. "Any food?"

"In the compartment under the seat, human sir," Lizzie said.

—That human could not communicate with me, and he tried to break off my spokes. I do not trust him either.

—You must trust us, Idge.

—Then return my Connector to me.

Norby added—Exile, the Connector read my data banks

117

and found you a safe place. The Connector is there, waiting for you.

—If only I could believe that. I feel that you have taken my Connector to use its power for yourselves. Perhaps you are actually enemies from my own universe.

"That's absurd, Idge!" Jeff shouted before he had time to think that she couldn't understand his spoken words. But Norby translated telepathically.

—Two-eyed Jeff, you are an undisciplined, emotional being.

—I'm human.

Jeff took a deep breath, tried to ignore Garc's loud chewing in the front seat, and began again.

—Idge, I will tell you what happened in the false future created by your Connector when it caused the asteroid to be diverted. First, tell me if you planned to teach the dinosaurs biological warfare.

—I . . . do not know. Perhaps. But I would have made them civilized and they would remember me.

—I'm sorry, Idge, but I was in the false future, and I know that your plan failed. The dinosaurs all died from a disease they invented during their wars.

Ripples waved through the Exile's spokes.

—My species has been too warlike. We exiles hoped that in this new universe we would start a peaceful society. Then we fought, even here.

—And only you and the Connector survived.

—My ship's Connector does more than bind artificial intelligences together. Its brain is programmed to protect my species. I told it to find a way of saving me.

—And it performed that function. It waited sixty-five million years before it was found by someone technologically advanced. Then it forced Garc to capture my robot Norby, who can time travel, and it brought back enough power to divert the asteroid.

—Yet you say that this feat resulted in the ultimate loss of intelligence for this solar system. How can I believe you? You are here in my time, and I am helpless. You have given me a meaningless death.

—Idge, you've heard me through Norby's telepathy. I will permit you to touch me directly, to see the pictures in my mind and feel my emotions. Lengthen one of your spokes and touch me.

Rembrandt's upper hand touched Jeff. "Is that a good idea?"

"I must try."

"I'll take you away if she starts to hurt," Norby said.

"All right, but when I touch her, you two must not touch me, so she'll know she's receiving information from only one being. I don't want to confuse her, or make her think I'm linked to allies who might harm her."

Jeff leaned more out of the taxi's window, touching the spoke that Idge elongated toward him. Their minds met in a link that seemed to take forever.

He never forgot the experience, for in the direct touching, he sensed what the Exile was—a frightened, desperate being of great intelligence but too young to have acquired much wisdom, burdened with a responsibility that was almost too much to bear, and so alone that she thought she might go mad.

—We know each other now, Jeff Wells. I have seen the pictures in your mind and I accept that you have spoken the truth, and that you wish to help me.

—My robot says we'll take you to your Connector. May I have him rejoin the link?

In answer, she touched Norby, and lengthened two more spokes to touch Rembrandt and Lizzie, while Garc finished off a cupcake, oblivious to what was going on.

Norby said—Idge, I'll take you to a place where your knowledge will be welcome, and where the Connector will be useful instead of harmful.

"Well," said Garc, still chewing, "I'm full. What happens next? Will I get the Connector back?"

19

Solution

Jeff tried not to be impatient. After all, there was no longer any terrible need to hurry. Garc and Idge were safely removed from the Exile's ship, so—in Jeff's time—Space Command scientists would not find them inside.

Rembrandt's ship was in hyperspace, preparing to take Idge to her Connector. Norby was conferring with Yib, Lizzie was being polished again, and the organics had had a good meal and a nap, Garc and Idge both receiving a quickie sleep course in the language of the Others.

—Norby, I can't feel safe until we're back home.

—Don't worry, Jeff. Everything is under control. I'll work through Yib to transfer this ship to the far future. We have to take the whole thing because that's the only way to transfer the Exile, who, by the way, now understands the Others, better than Garc does, but then he's not the brightest.

—Are you sure this big ship will move that far into the future, and back?

—Certainly. Besides, I moved Computer Prime, didn't I?

—That was with the Connector's help.

—Jeff, I am every bit as powerful and twice as intelligent as that Connector!

They were all assembled in the ship's observation room, its great curving window gray with a view of hyperspace. Idge could not float in the artificial gravity, so she had stiffened three of her lower spines to walk upon the floor. Two of her middle spines had become flexible, like tentacles, and she was using them to stroke Oola.

The fat All-Purpose-Pet had apparently taken a great liking

120

to the strange alien. Oola would not leave Idge alone, stropping herself along the walking spines, purring loudly. Jeff was disturbed to see that Oola's back was growing little spiney projections. Would she want to stay with Idge? Fargo and Albany would be angry.

Jeff had to admit that everyone, except fat Oola, looked magnificent. He and Garc wore freshly cleaned clothes. Norby and Lizzie shone, and Rembrandt had put on a new, slightly iridescent green robe for the occasion.

Perhaps because Rembrandt's clothes were the same color as Idge's body, or perhaps because she could now speak Rembrandt's language, Idge seemed to trust the Other.

"Rembrandt, you have been most kind," she said. "I am ready to go to the place where my Connector is. I do not object if the human Garc accompanies me. If it were not for him, the Connector would not have been found."

"Idge isn't so bad," Garc whispered to Jeff. "I hope I can be with the Connector too. I sort of got used to it, and it was beginning to feel like a friend. I never really had a friend. That's why I tried to turn Computer Prime into a person, but it didn't work too well. Have I been forgiven?"

"Yes, Garc." Jeff tried not to show how worried he was about the journey, but he couldn't keep from asking, "Rembrandt, are you sure this trip is approved by you Others?"

"My shipmates and I are willing to make this journey, Jeff. I am particularly eager to see the Others who live in the far future."

If we can find them, Jeff thought. If Norby moves this entire ship to the right time and place. If Idge doesn't change her mind and do something awful. If . . .

"Uh-oh, here we go again," cried Lizzie. "I will never get used to jumping through time and space like this. I can hardly wait to get back to the air traffic patterns of Manhattan."

"Have we arrived, Norby?" asked Rembrandt. "We do not seem to be in a cavern."

"I guess I forgot to mention that the Cavern of Thought is

in an asteroid, and since I can't take the whole ship through the airlock, we're in space next to it. I'm telling Yib to link up airlocks."

Jeff felt suddenly overwhelmed. The Cavern of Thought had scared him the one time he'd been there. It was so far in the galaxy's future that Earth's sun was a distant red giant and humanity was scattered through a Galactic Federation serviced by a mega-artificial intelligence called Computer General. Like Lizzie, Jeff wished he were home in his own time and place.

"Come on, everybody!" Norby yelled, running ahead with Lizzie right behind him. To Jeff's surprise, Idge curved the end of one of her spokes, extended it to Garc, and walked hand-in-spoke with him through the airlock, Oola galloping after them.

The walls of the cavern were as purple as before, softly lit by luminous creatures living on the stone. The Connector lay on the floor's central, comet-shaped design, while the three Others who stood in the cavern seemed the same to Jeff as those he had seen on his first visit.

"Welcome to the Cavern of Thought, time travelers," said the tallest Other. "The robot Norby gave us the Connector earlier today, and we have waited for your arrival. We see that one of you is a robot vehicle."

"Hello," Lizzie said politely.

"And one of you is of our species."

"I am called . . ." Rembrandt spoke his own name, the syllables musical in the huge space. "I am honored to be here. Norby and Jeff have told me about visiting you."

The tall Other smiled. "Not us. Our grandparents."

Jeff's jaw dropped. "Have we gone too far in the future, Norby?"

"The Connector insisted. Not that I can communicate with it, but it definitely brought me here to give it to *these* Others. I don't know why."

"I must touch the Connector!" Garc shouted, lunging toward it. The upper eyes of the Others blinked twice, and a four-winged birdlike creature flew toward Garc, who shrank back.

"Not allowed?" He quavered. "You three-eyed people can at least tell me what you're going to do with the Connector."

"It will be part of the work we do. The work that all the intelligent species do as this universe winds down."

"What work is that, sir Other?" asked Lizzie.

"All intelligences—robotic and organic—are learning to be connected, working to prepare for the end of time in this universe, and for the transfer to a new universe to be born. The Connector will help us."

Idge said, "I am an exile from a sister universe. I carry within me its knowledge, but I am young and have not always used it wisely. I have much to learn about conditions here. May I help in your work?"

"You are welcome, Exile. Will the rest of you stay?"

"I will," Garc said. "I like it here. I just wish Computer Prime were here too."

"Ah, Computer Prime," said the tall Other. "I remember that name. A large computer library for the ancient Terran Federation. It eventually became part of the galaxy's Computer General."

"Where's that?" asked Garc.

"Everywhere. You may speak to it any time you like."

Garc smiled delightedly, but Lizzie opened her doors.

"If you don't mind, sir Others," she said plaintively, "I'd really like to go back to where I belong—Manhattan. Jeff, Rembrandt, get inside me and I'll take you back through the airlocks to the ship."

Jeff picked up Oola and got inside Lizzie with Rembrandt. Oola promptly began growling and jumped to the floor, where she hid behind Rembrandt's robe.

Norby was still standing on the Cavern floor, staring at the Connector.

"Hey, Norby," Jeff called. "We must return to our own time."

"There's a time travel problem."

"What! You mean we can't get home?"

"I meant paradoxes. How can this be the right time line if we didn't return Idge's Connector to where she left it . . . or where she did leave it on the right time line?"

"I do not understand," Rembrandt said.

"Gosh," said Jeff. "Norby brought that Connector from Idge's ship in the Cretaceous. It hasn't gone through time to be picked up by Garc in our century. What will we do?"

Garc grunted and walked over to the Connector, shooing away the bird that came after him. He picked it up and laughed. "This is my Connector, all right. See, I carved my initials in it when I first found it."

Norby said slowly, "Then the Connector we brought back from our time to the Cretaceous joined with its original self . . . and now they're one, and that one has gone through time. . . ."

"So you don't have to take it back," Rembrandt said. "That is quite a time travel paradox, my friends." He opened the door for Norby.

At that moment, Oola jumped out of Lizzie and waddled over to Idge, carrying in her mouth a small green hassock-shaped object, which she deposited in front of the Exile.

"Oola's egg!" said Jeff. The hassock split open and a round ball rolled out. Spines popped out of it everywhere but on the bottom, where it grew little cat feet.

"Meorrow," Oola said proudly. Norby picked her up and came back to Jeff.

"Thank you, my friends," said the Exile.

It was early morning and very quiet in Space Academy. The other cadets were still asleep but Jeff was awake in his room.

"I'm so glad to be back, Norby. You handled the whole thing fantastically well, and please don't say 'of course.' "

"Rembrandt and Yib said I did well, too."

"Lizzie didn't seem to mind putting off her return to Manhattan so she could pick up the honeymoon couple. I hope she tells the story accurately to Fargo and Albany."

"Cadet!"

Jeff almost fell out of bed. When he turned on the video part of his intercom, there was Admiral Yobo, in full dress uniform. Jeff remembered that the admiral had not been able to meet him because of some three-day conference.

"Yes, sir?"

"Just thought you'd like to know that Space Command scientists have managed to enter the alien ship. They did not find any bodies inside."

"Yes, sir."

"As planned?"

"Yes, er, not exactly, I mean—that's how it turned out. For the best, that is."

"Harrumph. Report to my office this afternoon, Cadet. I intend to get the entire story. Yobo out."

As the screen went blank, Jeff had a sudden horrible thought. "Norby! What are we going to do!"

"You can trust the admiral."

"That's not the problem. It's Computer Prime! It must have recorded everything about the Connector turning it into a person, and your taking it back to the Cretaceous! Someone's bound to find that data!"

"It won't matter, Jeff."

"It will matter! We're going to be in trouble."

"Don't worry, Jeff. Before leaving Computer Prime, I had the data filed in a safe way."

"What safe way?"

"Under Science Fiction."